GHOSTS
IN WATERCOLOR

HOPE MILAM

FLASHPOINT
PUBLICATIONS

978-1-61929-517-9 Paperback
978-1-61929-518-6 ebook
978-1-61929-519-3 Hardback

Flashoint Publications First Edition: 2023

Printed in the United States of America.

www.flashpointpublications.com

Dedication

For Lane and Mr. Joe. May your memory be a blessing.

Chapter One

A loud bang caused my hand to jump, ruining what had been an almost straight line. I dropped the paintbrush and whirled around to look for the source of the noise. My heart was beating like a marching band doing triple time.

"Vinnie, did you knock something over?" My answer came a moment later when my muddled tiger striped cat ran through the room to hide under the bed. "Vinnie? Buddy? You okay?"

I can admit, since no one else was there, that I fell awkwardly to my knees. Vinnie was huddled in the far corner of the bed. I left him there. I knew that pose. He would be there for hours until he calmed down. Like cat, like human.

I got up and poured another whiskey and soda and looked back at my painting. I was thinking I could make that crazy line work when my cellphone rang. It was my mother's ring tone.

I lost a quick debate with myself and answered the phone. "Hi, Mom."

"Claire, hi. I didn't know if you'd answer the phone."

"What's up, Mom?" I was not in the mood to listen to her passive aggressiveness or the way she would gently berate me for not keeping in contact.

"Mr. Hawkins died this morning. The cancer finally got him." She sounded sad. I knew she had remained friends with the Hawkins family, but I also knew she was aware of my feelings on the matter.

"Why are you telling me this?" I dropped into my desk chair. I was not in the right headspace for this.

"I know you blame Mr. Hawkins for what happened to you, and to her, and I've never understood why. He was a big part of your life for so long, I thought you'd want to know. If you want to come down for the funeral, well, you can stay here like always." She never said her name, my mom, it was never Gwen. It was always a pronoun. It had always struck me as odd, but I let it go. I never questioned how people dealt with the world, post Gwen.

"I'll think about it, Mom."

"It's not like you have a real job or anything, I mean." She sighed. Maybe she heard my groan. "I just meant that you could do your art from anywhere."

"I know, Mom." My temples started throbbing. That was never a good sign. "Look, if I decide to come down. I'll let you know. Okay? I've got to go. I was right in the middle of another painting."

"Okay, I'll let you get back to that. Love you."

"Yeah." I put the phone down and sat back in my chair. "Son of a bitch."

Vinnie crept close, his one whole ear perked. What was left of the other one attempted to stand up. "I guess I need to find someone to watch you, buddy."

I told myself that I had not really decided if I was going to go. There was a good chance that Gabby would call, and she would talk me into it. I figured I could always cancel. Honestly, most people would expect me to flake out at the last minute. I had a history. My mother never failed to allude to it, but never went into detail.

The list of people I trusted to watch my cat was even shorter than the list of people who had my personal phone number. The sad part was I knew of exactly one person I could count on to take good care of my boy. The only problem was having to deal with her, or rather her current girlfriend. The main squeeze didn't like me. I honestly cannot say I blame her, I was a shitty girlfriend. Hell, I was a shitty friend. I had been reminded of that many times.

Resigned and desperate, I picked up the phone again after quickly downing my drink. I needed something to firm up my resolve. If there had been a death though, that meant a funeral and mourning and stuff. I felt that should at least count for something. Funerals were usually emotional events. I thought maybe I could get her to agree out of sympathy. It was manipulative and probably wrong, but I didn't feel bad about it. I had too much other guilt I was carrying to let that hitch a ride with all my other baggage.

"What?" April sounded annoyed when she answered, surprised she answered instead of letting it go to voicemail. Of the few times I had reached out since our parting, she had done that, let it go and then text me later. She didn't like speaking to me or hearing my voice. Probably reminded her of our breakup or something.

"Hi. Look, I know it's very short notice, but I have to fly home. There's been a death and I need to go to the funeral." I tried to sound pathetic. I spoke quickly, as well. I wanted to finish what I had to say before she could interject something, change the topic to something really unpleasant, like why our relationship ended.

"I'm sorry to hear that." Her concern was genuine. It almost made me feel bad about the whole situation. "You need someone to watch our cat?"

"He's not..." I stopped. The quickest way to piss her off would have been to argue with her. Even though I had found Vinnie two years prior to our relationship, April still insisted on shared ownership. For a long moment after we parted ways, it scared me she would file for custody. "Yes. Can you please watch Vinnie? You know how he hates flying."

"Oh, my God! She laughed. "I thought we were going to get kicked off that flight. Sorry. Family?" I could still hear the smile on her face.

"What?" It caught me off guard. The laugh had been so free and easy. It brought to mind somewhat happier days.

"Was it a family member? Your mom is okay, right?" She had liked my mother. Mom had liked April, too. I don't remember how she felt about my father. To be fair, half the time I didn't remember how I felt about the man.

"They're fine, my parents. I'll probably stay with them." I rubbed my head. It was aching. "Thanks for doing this. Should I drop him off or do you want to pick him up?"

"Um." She paused. It was a tough question. I was not welcome at their apartment. Shelly would shoot on sight and I wasn't sure how good her aim was. "I'll text you a time and place we can meet. How's that?" I resisted the urge to scoff. It hurt.

"That's fine. Thanks." I sighed, filled with relief for finding a safe place for Vinnie to be while I was away. I knew if something happened, if I didn't make it back, he would have a good life with April, even with Shelly there. I mean just because the woman hated me didn't make her a bad person. It made her smart in my opinion.

"When are you leaving?" She didn't seem to be in a hurry to disconnect. It struck me as odd, and then I realized she needed more information. She couldn't just read my mind and get details about when I needed Vinnie at her place.

"The first flight I can get." I answered honestly. I had not yet even looked at airline reservations.

"Gabby going with you?

"I don't know. I haven't talked to her about it."

"I'm sure you will." I knew that tone. That was the unhappy April tone.

"April, I—" She had always been jealous of Gabby for some reason.

"Okay. Take care, Claire. I'll text you a time and place." She cut off whatever I was going to say. That was good because I hadn't thought of a reply.

"Gotcha. Thanks." I disconnected, having no desire for more awkward conversation.

I had wanted it to be different with April. I wanted it to be more like it was with Gabby. Sadly, it was not. April had insisted on staying in contact after the breakup, despite my objections, and really the objections of everyone we knew. At least she had agreed to watch him. It was not more than a thirteen-hour drive home, but I really didn't want to make it if I didn't have to. Flying was intrusive and scary, but I preferred it to driving long distances.

My head was killing me! The pounding started in my temples with the first call and just steamrolled on in. I tossed my phone and my glasses on the desk and headed to the shower. On the way I grabbed a few aspirin and chewed those while undressing. The bitter taste was familiar and reassuring. It was a habit I had picked up in school after reading about a character who did the same.

I let the water run as hot as possible before stepping in and letting the spray hit the crown of my head and fall to my shoulders. It felt almost as if it was melting the pain away. I could feel the tight cords in my shoulders relax into something vaguely resembling human muscles. It was amazing how tight everything had gotten from one phone call.

When the water started running warm, I washed and got out, almost tripping over Vinnie in the process. He liked to sit just outside the shower door and watch to make sure I didn't drown. I dried off and pulled on my robe. I lived alone, but modesty was still a hard habit to break. The phone was ringing again when I returned to the living area.

"What's up, Gabby?" Like my mom, Gabby also had her own ringtone. It really helped me screen calls.

"Have you heard? Hawkins is dead." Typical Gabby. She bypassed greetings and got straight to the point.

"Yeah, I know. Mom already called me."

"I just literally hung up with my sister two minutes ago and then called you, and your mother still beat me to it."

"Literally two minutes?" I asked. Gabby was not one to confuse literally and figuratively.

"Yes. I hung up, got a drink and then called." I heard her exasperated sigh though she tried to hide it. "Are you going down there?"

"Yeah. I guess. Maybe. I mean, I got April to watch Vinnie. I was about to pack and make plane reservations." The pain in my head started again, and I was confused. Last minute reservations were hard to cancel. Maybe I really did intend to go.

"You don't want to drive?" It was easy to detect the hopefulness in her tone. Gabby hated flying.

"Sorry, Gabs. You know I hate road trips." That was true. I never saw the appeal in the idea. "And seriously, I'm not sure I'm going."

"But Claire, come on."

I heard a ding in my ear.

"Shit, hang on." I held the phone away and looked at the screen. The alert was a four-word response from April.

Sorry. Can't. Next time.

"Fuck."

"What was that?" I heard chewing. She tried to talk around it. It was slightly annoying.

"April." The pain was getting intense again. I really wanted another drink.

"Shelly vetoed the idea of helping you?" Gabby asked after a pause. I assumed she swallowed whatever she had been eating. It was probably one of those herbal vitamin supplements she took like candy.

"Apparently. Okay. Be ready tomorrow morning. Early." I sighed. "When I decide not to go, I'll text you."

"How early is that?" she asked. She ignored the rest of what I said. Gabby was not an early morning person, which made sense since she worked nights.

"It's about a four-hour drive from me to you." I was mentally calculating the best I could around the pain. "I should be there no later than ten. I'll call on the way, okay? If I decide to go. You know I haven't decided yet, right?"

"Okay. I'll call Zu. Do you want to meet with the others?" She always ignored my protests to get me to go to things. It's like she knew I couldn't say no to her.

"Damn it, Gabby. You just assume I'm going? I have a life here, you know." Anger bubbled up through the pain in my head.

"I know. And I know you're going. You're going to get off the phone with me, call or text Lane, pack up your stuff and then see me tomorrow. I get the lovely opportunity to talk to my boss to get time off. I never take it, but I bet you a buck fifty they'll have a problem with it. So, want me to call the others?"

"You think they'll come down?" The five of us, the survivors, had not been together in a long time. As a rule, we tried to avoid one another, or maybe that was just me. I was not certain.

"Yeah, I'm pretty sure. I mean it's Hawkins." She spoke with an affection I didn't feel. It was the same tone she used when she talked about her parents. I knew it well. Despite what had happened to us, to Gwen, Gabby's parents were still close to her.

"True. Yeah. I don't mind. Just the five of us, right, the survivors?" There were not many people I spoke to from my high school days. After Gwen disappeared, I was pretty much ostracized. The others, too, Gabby, Zubieda, Silas, and Oliver.

"Like anyone else wants to remember we exist," she said. It was true. Just the rumors around that accident, and us, were enough to keep the town talking for years. "I'll see you in the morning, Claire. Thanks."

"Don't thank me. Thank Shelly. It's her fault I'm driving." If nothing else, at least I would have company I could tolerate on the way.

"Yeah, but you should have Vinnie with you. That damned cat is your familiar. You don't want to be without him." I could hear the lighter and her first breath of cigarette smoke.

"You know I don't believe that hippy, Wicca crap." I didn't bust her for smoking. We all reacted differently to stress. "Get some rest, Gabs. I'll see you in the morning."

"You, too."

The rest of the day was a waste, I could tell. I had lost the ability to concentrate. The work in progress could wait, as could the background for the graphic novel I was doing for Lane. He would understand, or not. I took a few moments and fired off texts to my mother telling her I would soon inhabit the guest cottage and to Lane telling him I would be out of town for a few days. I texted my landlord the same.

Then it was time to pack. I decided to wait until morning to pack Vinnie's stuff. He tended to get excited whenever he thought he was going for a ride. I often wondered if he was part dog, but my veterinarian laughingly assured me that was impossible. Still, I thought it was odd for a cat to like riding in the car.

I sat on the edge of the bed and stared around my apartment. It was small, but it was private, and it was mine. But my past had followed me here. It lived with me, an annoying ghost with my best friend's face. It was going to be a long night.

My name is Claire Susan Evans, I told myself. And I am a survivor. I just don't remember what I survived.

Chapter Two

One thing I liked about the club Lane had chosen is it was loud. There was usually a deejay and pounding dance music. It made a great place to be where the burdens of conversation were lifted. That was how it usually was. It was different this time.

"What's with all the quiet?" I asked. I couldn't believe I had decided to meet him. After I packed and was ready to drink myself to sleep, he had called and requested that I meet him here. I don't know why I agreed.

"It's always like this on Tuesdays. It makes for a nice change." He pushed a glass across the table to me. His bright red shirt was louder than the room. Of course, that was one thing I liked about Lane. For all his creative talent as a writer, he wore bright colors instead of the stereotypical black and gray.

"It's not what I was expecting."

"No? You usually hate loud noises."

"I do. I just felt like getting lost in the noise and alcohol tonight. I thought that's what you were offering." It's why I had agreed to meet him. At art school we had gone out and hung around loud bars and judged people. It had been fun.

"Look, I detected a tone in your attitude when you texted me. What's going on?"

"What do you mean?" My senses turned on high alert.

"I mean you seemed distracted and a bit like you were when we first met."

"I thought we agreed you wouldn't remind me of that." I stirred my drink around, wishing I could down it like I normally would if I was alone. When I had met Lane, I had not been in a good place mentally or emotionally. Honestly, I couldn't remember a time when I had been in a place like that.

"I'm just saying I could feel the struggle. What's got you so freaked?" He leaned a little closer and tried to catch my gaze.

"I'm not freaked." I thought my acting skills had gotten better. Apparently, I was wrong. I downed the drink and waved for a server. I was going to need so many more.

"We're up for an award, you know that right?" At least his smile was bright and genuine. He was rightfully proud of that achievement.

"Yeah, I saw the email you sent." It didn't impress me. I knew he deserved it. Lane was an amazing writer, but I was only an average illustrator.

"And you sold that painting for a shit ton of money. You should be happy, on top of the world, and everything." He shrugged.

I always hated those assumptions that success would lead to happiness.

"You would think." The first server ignored me. Tempted to put up a white flag, I surrendered to the need for alcohol. "You want anything else?"

"Already? I can't keep up with you. One glass and I'm about done. I thought you were out after two, but I'll try. I don't want to leave you drinking alone." He turned in his seat and waved a server to our table.

"That never works for me here," I complained.

"That's because they're usually straight. Honestly, you look pretty femme anyway. Sitting here with me, I bet people think we're on a date."

"You think? Really?" It was strange. I never really thought other people saw me as anything more than weird, with long dark hair that had absolutely no body to it and dark eyes full of sadness, bordering on madness. At least that was according to an ex-girlfriend. She was why I decided never to date writers, as they're wordy and pretentious. "I'll take a double and bring another in a few minutes. My friend here is paying."

"I'm paying?" Lane looked at the server. "I guess I'm paying. We wouldn't be up for an award without her art."

"You're the artist?" The server finally acknowledged me. I guess I mattered now that I did something more than take up space at her table.

"I am. I do the art for Lane's graphic novels."

"That is so cool. I'll go get your drinks." She hurried off. I took a moment to appreciate the good view as she did so.

"She'll have her thighs wrapped around your head if you wink at her," Lane said.

"I don't know. Women are crazy. People are crazy." I looked down at the rapidly melting ice in my glass. It would have made a gorgeous still life. "Maybe it's me."

"Are you okay? You're not, are you?" He put a slightly calloused hand on mine. I felt so aware of every little thing and yet so blind. So very blind.

"That your pencil hand? Your fingers are calloused."

"I know. My wife keeps telling me to use lotion, but I don't listen. I don't like the way it feels." Lane's voice always seemed to hold a hint of amusement. It was if he really enjoyed life. I didn't get it.

"That's crazy."

"What is? You're not back on the *you're too talented and neat to be straight* thing, are you?"

It was an old joke. I didn't find it funny this time.

"No. Love who you love." I shrugged. The night was not getting better. I rubbed my head, trying vainly to make the ache inside go away.

"Seriously, Claire. What is going on?"

"I have to go out of town for a funeral." I knew the power of those words. People cut slack for someone in mourning where they wouldn't otherwise.

"I'm so sorry. Who died?" He stopped for a second and bowed his head. "That was a rude question. Sorry."

"Mr. Hawkins died." I moved back and allowed the server to place the drinks on the table.

"Five minutes, right?" she asked. She didn't even glance at Lane this time.

"Please. Thanks." I blinked against the lights. They seemed to get brighter and a little streaky.

"Who was Mr. Hawkins? His death seems to have really put you in a tailspin. What's wrong?"

"Nothing's wrong. I'm just going to go stay at my parents for a few days and make sure that the bastard is really dead." After it came out of my mouth, I regretted the words, but only because I knew it would lead to more questions.

"Okay, so that sounds like there's some major backstory there. Who was he?"

"Damn, Lane. You're usually not this invasive."

He had learned early in our partnership not to ask personal questions.

"And you're usually not drinking this much, especially like this on a random Tuesday."

He had no idea. Long ago I had learned to do the majority of my drinking at home. It was cheaper and way less stressful. The more one drank in public, the more people noticed and commented.

"Mr. Hawkins was my band director in high school." I hadn't told Lane the story. Hell, I hadn't told anyone the story. I wasn't even sure what the story was, and I was in it.

"And why does that make you hate him? Let me guess? Wool uniforms in southern summer heat? You know, that would make me hate someone." He shrugged. "I wasn't in band, but my wife has stories."

"I don't remember much." I finished my second drink. "Has it been five minutes yet?"

"Isn't this a bit much for you, Claire?" Lane's face was growing a bit fuzzy, but not enough. "I mean, I rarely drink, and you don't very often. We had a glass or two of wine after the publication of the first book, but this is not you."

"How do you know?" I snapped. I didn't know myself, so how could anyone else? That anger I had felt on the phone with Gabby was back.

"We've met. Does this have something to do with the unresolved childhood trauma you've got?" Like Gabby, he ignored the anger.

"What?" I almost dropped my drink. There were certain things I didn't talk about, and that was a big one. "What are you talking about?"

"Claire, seriously." He sighed, leaned back and looked directly at me. "I guess you don't trust me, and that's okay. My wife is a trauma survivor. I know it's difficult. If this guy, your band director, was involved in it, maybe you should go to his funeral. Seeing his corpse might bring you peace. But you at least owe it to yourself to try healing. This could be a step toward that."

"You have no idea." How could he? I didn't.

"No, I don't. You've never told me, but it seeps out. It's in your drawings, your web comic, your painting, In everything. Like I said, I've seen it enough to know you've had some serious shit happen to you. Becca, she's been through—" He paused and looked away for a brief second. Well, I won't break her confidence, but she's been through some shit. I hold her through it. I've helped her though it. I've watched, helpless, as she's dealt with it. It's not easy, but she's in a much better space than she was when we got together. A support group, a good group of friends, an amazing therapist, and some high-quality medication have really made a difference for her. But it all started when she wanted it bad enough to do it."

"I need to go. Thanks for the drinks."

I couldn't do it anymore. I couldn't stay there and listen to someone who had no idea. There was a reason I didn't have many friends. Friends meant closeness and sharing, and I couldn't do that. It, what happened, drove a wedge into everything in my life. There were people I hung out with, but it was all surface level. I had a group of people that I went to bars and clubs with when I wanted to be somewhere loud and obnoxious. I didn't consider them friends, simply acquaintances.

I left him there. I didn't turn around. I didn't want to see the look of disappointment I knew would be there. I was very familiar with it. I saw it all the time on both Gabby and my mother's faces.

I drove home in silence with that old song going through my head questioning if I should stay or if I should go. It was not until I was almost asleep that night that I sent a text to Gabby telling her to be ready to be picked up the next morning. She sent back a thumbs up emoji. At least she didn't rub it in.

It was almost past midnight when I realized I had not eaten. I was not in the mood for food, so I drank my calories. I had suffered from headaches since I was eighteen and no one could find the cause of them. However, through a lot of trial and error I had found a way to lessen the pain. Two muscle relaxers and several shots of vodka was the recipe. After that, it was lights out and remaining horizontal for a few hours with an ice pack on my head, and a washcloth near my nose in case it started bleeding. It had only done that once when I had the flu, but I felt it was better to be prepared.

I didn't want to think. In fact, I tried to keep my mind empty by concentrating solely on the warmth the vodka had created in my belly and the cold of the ice. Tonight, though, I could not help wondering why I would want to make sure Hawkins was dead when everyone else practically worshipped the man. It made no sense. Finally, I chalked it up to more of that time period I could not remember, even though I was not sure how our band director could have been involved in a boating accident. The puzzle followed me into my dreams. It was another night of not enough sleep and too many dreams.

Chapter Three

I woke the next morning to an angry cat and a sour stomach.

Fortunately, I hadn't much of a hangover so I guess practice really does make perfect. I'd had a lot of practice.

It was early, before sunrise. After feeding the cat, I loaded the car and gave him a few minutes for his morning routine. I didn't pack a litter box for the car. I didn't know if they even made those, much less did I want to know. It didn't matter. I had an extra one at my parents' house.

Vinnie was safely in his crate when I placed him in the car. It was still early enough to beat commuter traffic. I stopped through a drive through and loaded up on coffee and a bad breakfast. It would hold me until Memphis when I would collect Gabby. We could grab lunch there.

Once on the highway, I let Vinnie out of his cage. He loved lying in the back window getting sun and watching the passing cars. I also turned on an audio book. I hated having to find radio stations constantly when traveling. The sound of static put my teeth on edge and usually started a headache. I had a lot of audio books, but I usually stayed with one or two. It was hard to find a good narrator, at least for me it was.

I made it to Gabby's apartment building in a little less than four hours. It was not a bad time considering the amount of road construction I passed. I texted her to let her know I was there and then put a harness and leash on Vinnie. I usually got strange looks when I walked the cat, but I could hardly expect him to hold his bladder for the entire trip.

Really, I didn't walk him like he was a dog. I didn't keep him at my side and make him heel. I used a retractable leash and stayed in one spot. He got to explore and the leash was more to ensure his return than anything. By the time Gabby had put her bag in the back seat, we were ready to hit the road.

"Dude, stop by a gas station or something. I need snacks and coffee. And for fuck's sake, can we get rid of the book on tape shit?" Gabby demanded as soon as she opened the passenger side door.

"You're in a good mood this morning," I observed. Gabby was not a morning person.

"I slept like shit last night. I went to work, told them what was going on. Do you know they didn't want to let me take the personal time? I never take time off. Anyway, the big boss had to get involved, and she was not happy she had to be woken up for it. We'd been through hell together when she worked nights at the ER before she got promoted, so she knew me. Long story short, I got a paid week off. Of course, I still have like a month of vacation and personal time left." She got an audio cord out of her bag and plugged her phone into my stereo's aux input. "Don't worry. Static free."

"Thanks." I turned back onto the highway and looked around for a decent looking gas station. "You sure you don't want fast food of some sort?"

"Seriously? Fuck no. You know those places use animal products in everything." She side eyed me. "Hopefully, a decent gas station will have something I can choose from."

"You going to be okay with coffee not harvested to your specifications?" I teased. My friend was one of the most principled people I knew, but it was fun to tease her about it.

"Shit, Claire. Don't be a bitch. I have standards, but I also know that it's not always easy to drink by them." She stuck her tongue out at me. "We've got seven hours in this car. Lighten up."

"I slept like shit, too," I told her. We knew one another too well to pretend around one another.

"I can tell. What helped you get to sleep this time?" Gabby was a nurse and knew a little too much about my self-medicating practices. She didn't always agree with them. However, I always wondered if the choices she made to cope were an attempt to assuage her guilt differently than the way I did. We all had to cope somehow.

"I had one of those headaches again," I explained. I knew she would understand. Like me, she also had a constant, recurring ailment that started at eighteen. She had problems with her ears. She was prone to insane earaches that left her dizzy and nauseous. It was one reason she hated to fly. Her earaches were also a mystery, not for lack of trying, but there was no medical explanation. As a result, Gabby was well versed in supplements, plant extracts, holistic medicines, and all sorts of new age non-pharmaceutical stuff to ease her symptoms. The only problem with that was she had always seemed to suffer from one ailment or another. She was essentially a holistic hypochondriac.

"Fuck. Was it the news?" She sniffed a couple of times. I didn't look, accustomed to her behavior. I would have bet she had some sort of inhaler and was squirting organic mist up her nose.

"Beats the hell out of me." I barely kept from snapping. Instead, I shrugged and guided the car into a parking space in front of a large gas station. She was my best friend. We had been through too much together to argue. Even when our brief fling ended, it had been extremely civil. Like the only thing that changed was we didn't sleep with one another after it.

"Don't you need gas?" Gabby asked.

"Shit. Yeah." I sighed and put the car in reverse but didn't move it. "Look, go on in. I'll fuel up and meet you inside. I could certainly do with a refill." My brain was sluggish. I needed caffeine. It's like I was moving through a fog in slow motion.

"No worries." She hopped out of the car as soon as I stopped it. "I'll catch the next tank, okay?"

"Sure. Thanks."

I waited until her door was closed and backed into a spot near the fuel pumps, pleased that at least I had remembered which side the gas tank was on. I pushed my sunglasses on top of my head, got the nozzle in the right way, and patiently waited for the fuel to start.

"Ma'am?" A large man in a larger truck got my attention.

"Yes?" At least I was not rude.

"It's beeping. Maybe it didn't take your card," he suggested.

"What?" I looked at it in irritation. He was right. The pump had not started because I had not inserted my card to begin with. "Yeah, it didn't. Thanks."

"No problem." He seemed cautious about speaking to me. I guess I still looked out of sorts. Plus, I was in my road trip outfit, which is the same thing I usually wore when I painted, yoga pants, flats, and an oversized t-shirt heavy with paint stains and emblazoned with some has been band's logo. I had a hatred of sneakers and socks, wearing both only when I had no other option. In short, I'm sure I looked as if I'd been dragged through hell.

At least I had my hair in a clip instead of letting it fly where it wanted to go. It was past my shoulders at that point and my bangs were in the process of growing out from a ridiculous haircut choice. I looked as if I had just left an all-night theme party, and the theme was crazy sorority hag or hungover yoga mom.

I took care of the payment and selected the correct grade fuel and got the whole process started. Then I could lean back on the car and let my mind just exist for a few minutes. Though I had felt the buzzing of a headache periodically that morning, it was still at bay. I desperately wanted a drink but pulling out a flask and upending it while putting gas in my car would have been a bad idea. I needed to wait until I was safely out of sight from everyone, especially from any cops in the area.

I didn't want to curse myself into a headache, so I cast around to think of something else. What came to mind was my traveling companion. Gabriella Rodriguez. She was the only person I still talked to from high school. She kept up with the other four, but Gabby was my only contact with them, unless Silas was in one of his moods and reached out to me.

Honestly, I think she was their only point of contact for me as well.

It's funny. In high school, Gwen had been my best friend. Actually, Gwen had been my best friend since preschool, I'm sure. We had even planned to go to the same college, but after the accident, things changed. Gwen was no longer around, and I took a year off and tried to disappear. Gabby found me and convinced me to go to college. I did. So did she. I went to art school. She climbed the nursing ladder until she was a nurse practitioner. Somewhere along the way we had become professionals who tried hard to adult like normal people.

Gabby, for all five foot two feet of her, was pure heart. She was sometimes loud and liked head banger music, but she was loyal and very forgiving to those she considered friends. I think, despite everything else, at least I am fortunate enough to be counted as one of those. No matter what I did, no matter what I said, or how I treated her, she stuck by me.

The nozzle clicked and startled me. I replaced it and moved the car back in front of the gas station. I hated when people just left their cars there like no one else wanted to get gas. Gabby was waiting for me inside.

"Okay, I managed to find hummus, trail mix and raisins." She held up her haul. "What are you getting?"

"I don't know. Probably chips and a candy bar." I shrugged. I was not terribly fond of food, or so I had convinced myself once. I ate because I was hungry, but I never went out of my way to get food I enjoyed. I did, however, have a fondness for a certain candy bar with nougat and caramel.

"Bloat city." She rolled her eyes. "I'll get your coffee unless you want a soda?"

"No sugar, two creams. Please." I watched for a moment as she deposited the stuff on the counter and sauntered off to get the coffee.

I made a quick trip to the restroom both to relieve my bladder and have a few shots of whisky. I could only shoot vodka if it was cold. After returning to the main store area, it only took a few minutes before

I had picked out my beloved candy bar, a bag of chips and two bottles of water. I could not live by coffee alone.

"There's a cat in that car outside." An older woman with internet famous hair announced as she entered.

"Yeah. We'll be out in a minute," I told her. It wasn't hot outside, and the car was in the shade. I had even cracked the windows, but I was sure Vinnie was safe from harm.

"You ought to be ashamed of yourself," the woman told me. "I should call the cops."

"Lady, they haven't been here ten minutes," the young man behind the counter informed her.

"That's right." Gabby walked up, pocketing her change. "We're just about to leave, as soon as my friend pays for her junk food. Vinnie is perfectly safe."

"Still." The woman looked her up and down with a very clear look of distaste on her face and a little bit of self-righteousness in her stance

"Go on and crank the car." I tossed Gabby the keys. There was still something of a firebrand in my friend and I didn't want a misguided woman in a gas station to experience it.

"Fine." She hefted her bag and headed out the door.

"I can't even." The woman seemed at a loss for words.

"I know," I reassured her. Gabby was extremely professional and in her scrubs you would never know that the emergency room nurse was heavily tattooed. The pentacle on her forearm usually threw people off when they saw it. "It's okay."

"Is this all for you?" the young man asked. It took me a second to puzzle out his meaning.

"Yes. That's everything." I watched him bag everything and then swiped my card. It was with relief that I made it to the car.

"Some people." It was the only thing my friend said as we turned back onto the highway to continue our journey.

We stopped once more on the way to Bayview for gas, more snacks and the restroom. No one accosted us this time and I remembered to pay before trying to start the pump. Gabby offered, but I declined. I liked to keep the receipts for tax purposes. It was not easy working freelance. I needed every tax deduction I could get even after my recent so-called success. Instead, I let her buy the snacks.

We made it to Bayview before dinnertime. I dropped Gabby off at her mother's house and then headed home. My parents were not there. I didn't expect them to be, honestly. I was glad, too. I was able to put my stuff away in the little apartment behind the house and get Vinnie situated before I heard one of their cars in the driveway.

I would let them come to me. I was too tired and raw to impose my company upon them. I checked the fridge and found a few pre-made dinners my mother must have placed there. My mother was not the best cook but eating the food she had left for me was comforting. I ate half of one before falling into an uneasy self-medicated sleep on the bed.

Chapter Four

What woke me the next morning was a loud banging on the door. I stumbled to my art portfolio and fumbled for the lock. My mother was not the person I wanted to see before I became fully coherent. She was absolutely brilliant, a retired marine botanist, but always had been a little cold and reserved.

"Mom?"

"I was going to come see you last night when I got home but thought it best to let you get some rest." She edged past me and entered the little room.

The apartment was a one-room efficiency my father had built for his mother several years ago. It was the only place on the property where I felt comfortable. It had a small stove, a fridge, a tiny sink, a mere slice of counter space, as well as a standup shower and toilet in the lone bathroom. The bathroom was the only room that had privacy. The bed was against one wall and the dining table was opposite it. You had to sit on the bed or in the solitary chair to watch television. I didn't mind though. I rarely watched TV.

"It was a long drive," I answered.

"I'm surprised you didn't fly down. I could have met you at the airport." Like most of her reprimands, this was gentle and almost unnoticeable. It was almost as if she had practiced at being human.

"I know. Gabby and I decided to drive instead." I didn't tell her the real reason. My mother had been great before the accident, despite her more reserved nature. Afterwards, she seemed an embarrassed stranger. I honestly am not sure which one of us changed more.

"Ah. So, Gabriella is home, too?" My mother had never liked my friends, except for Gwen. Everyone had liked Gwen. Even before the accident, Gwen had been everyone's favorite. She had been a good person and a good friend. Her disappearance made her a saint.

"Yes. We're going to the funeral. The guys and Zu will be here, too." I set out all the bad news for her at one time.

"How nice." Her voice faltered. "I see you're alone here."

"Yes. Still single, Mother." I rubbed my left temple. It was stinging a little right inside it.

"I wouldn't know. You barely talk to me, you shut me out." She turned toward the door. "Maybe it's because of your father. Maybe it's me. I don't know."

"Mother." This was both unfair and untrue. At least I thought it was. I remember it being the other way around. I could have been wrong, however. It would not have been the first time. My life and the way I remembered it always seemed a little surreal. "I'm fine. Everything's cool."

"The ladies' club would like you to do a little presentation while you are home. Any thoughts on how long you'll be here?" Sometimes I really did get the feeling that she was trying to bridge whatever gap was between us but didn't know how. I didn't know either. Whatever had happened to us was too vague for support groups.

"I haven't given it a thought," I answered honestly. There were not many things in my life I planned, not even when I had been a kid. That always bothered her. My mother was a big planner, being one of those naturally analytical people. It seriously was annoying. But it was how she was.

"Well, after you sold that painting and it was in the magazines and all, they asked if you'd want to do a little social gathering." The club she belonged to was more a gardening club than anything. I didn't remember them ever having a social, public thing. Then again, I never paid much attention to it.

"Maybe." I would follow that up later. I would need more information and booze before agreeing to sit around and talk art with a bunch of little old gardeners, intent on cross breeding the perfect cabbage flower or whatever it was they were on about. Plants were not my thing. I didn't even like painting them. It was just one more thing my mother and I did not have in common.

"I'm not sure I like or even understand the piece, but it did sell for a lot, didn't it?" she stated in awe. It was as if it had finally hit her, one could make money doing art.

"I guess." I had sold a few paintings here and there from the time I was in art school, but this past one had been a shocker. I'd had it on consignment in a gallery in Chicago and the astute gallery owner had gotten so many inquiries, she had fostered a bidding war. Together we made a little more than a million dollars. That was after taxes of course. Then of course, I had to pay her commission.

"Yes, well, they were all impressed." She sighed when I didn't respond. "It's nice to be able to brag on you, you know."

"Really?" I didn't want the answer. "I'm going to change and go for a run. Is Mabel's still serving breakfast?"

"Of course," she said. "Are you sure you don't want donuts?"

"I'm sure." I scowled. Mabel's was one of the local diners and served a decent breakfast. People who would never join my mother's garden club also frequented it. "I'll see you later, Mom."

"Okay. Let me know about the thing. They need an answer tomorrow," she said, closing the door behind her.

"Of course, they do," I muttered after she was gone.

I had started running in art school. The aftermath of the accident, or incident, whichever I felt like calling it at any given time, was an increased desire for comfort food. In hard contrast to the current day, back then, when I was all of nineteen, food was an enormous deal. It didn't matter what it was, I would have third helpings of it. A therapist had suggested it resulted from being shipwrecked and missing for three days. She was sure we had not eaten at all in that time. She had suggested running as a means to combat the excess poundage until we got the overeating under control. We never did.

A few years after art school, when I was working as a graphic designer for a small firm in St. Louis, I stopped eating altogether. I was young and single and fat artists didn't get many dates, nor could I afford too much food with student loans, rent and other bills due. My past therapist and I came to a compromise. I eat until I am full. I run every day. I skip a few meals and a few runs. I do fudge that a little. There are nights when I drink my dinner. Vodka is made from potatoes and whiskey is made from some sort of grain, right? That has to count for something. Regardless, it kept me alive and at a size or two larger than I'm supposed to wear according to fashion magazines and modern standards. I had curves. That I was okay with.

I thought about all that as I dressed for my run. It had been a long time since I had willingly run through the streets of my hometown. I honestly could not remember the last time. Perhaps that had been when I had come home for my grandmother's funeral. It seemed a funny coincidence. Death kept dragging me back to this town that I wanted to avoid more than anything.

My mother still lived in the house in which I was raised. It is downtown and close to most everything but the new schools they had to build. I warmed up on the oak shaded sidewalks, the concrete broken and jagged in places. The streets were asphalt and old, faded to a dark gray rather than black. Downtown was not as an attractive an address as it once was.

Most of the bars and restaurants are still downtown though. Everything else had long since crept to the town's borders where there was more room. I easily fell into a nice rhythm, watching for cars and keeping my eyes in front of me. I never knew if I would be recognized. Bayview had grown exponentially, but someone always seemed to remember that ill-fated trip and the mystery surrounding the one kid who didn't make it back.

Mabel's was older than I. I think it was older than my grandfather. It was a small diner with an all-day breakfast menu and a twenty-four-hour schedule. It was a favorite hangout as a teenager. I noticed as I approached that apparently it was still the place where most of the city eats breakfast. At least those who didn't want sugar laden dough, cook at home, or deal with the Arnoux family drama.

At first it went pretty well. I took a seat in the counter's corner area and perused the menu. The server took my order and supplied me with coffee. I even found a newspaper someone left at the counter. I was skimming through the Bayview Monitor looking mainly at the headlines, trying to see if I recognize any of the bylines and looking for the obituaries when I heard loud whispering behind me.

"I'm sure it is," one person said.

"Nah, aren't they all dead now?" another voice asked.

"No, just the one died, the one they killed out on that island."

It never failed. If I returned to Bayview, someone thought they knew who I was, and the whispering would start. Fortunately, a distraction happened as the server set down my plate. My phone rang.

"Hello?"

"Claire, how you feeling this morning?" Gabby didn't sound cheerful.

"Well, I'm sitting at Mabel's trying to eat breakfast," I said loudly. "And an old couple behind me are wondering if we killed Gwen. What about you?" The whispering behind me stopped and I chanced a quick look at them. It was an older couple, and they were both staring determinedly at their coffees.

"I got that same stare down at the café."

If I closed my eyes, I could see her roll hers.

"Don't they fry their donuts in animal fat?" I asked around a mouth full of egg. Gabby was usually easy to tease, provided I stayed away from her holistic self-medicating habit. She never owned up to that. Her denials were not convincing.

"Nope. Vegetable oil. I double-checked. Have you heard from anyone else?"

"You are the only one I talk to, you know that," I reminded her again. "Too bad you don't like meat. This ham is excellent."

"Just because some assholes recognized you, don't tease me with food. Ham is still pig." She stopped her indignant rant, which was disappointing. It was always fun to get Gabby going. "Anyway, we're meeting at Myles's at seven for drinks. Did you want to grab dinner beforehand?"

"What's Myles's?" It was new to me. Most of the old restaurants were gone. Newer and supposedly hipper places had opened in their stead. Mabel's, Arnoux's and the café were the only ones left I recognized.

"Some burger and beer joint down on Main. It's supposed to be good." I heard someone talk to her in the background. Her answer to them was too muffled for me to hear. "So, want to meet first?"

"Yeah, we can do that. I'm always down for a good burger." It was one thing I still savored, along with the candy bar. "Want me to pick you up?"

"Yeah. That'd be great." Gabby's propensity for vertigo made her unable to drive cars legally. She didn't seem to mind. Even though Memphis didn't have the best public transport in the country, she got around. She biked a lot.

"Cool. I'm going to finish my ham and eggs and then jog back home. I'll see you around six, okay?"

"Okay. Don't kill the old folks. You know they don't get it." She spoke from experience. It plagued us all, and it was easier to let it slide rather than examine anything.

"I know, but the sad part is we don't either." That bothered me more than it had before. For the first time in a long time, I could feel curiosity growing under the unease I had in Bayview. Maybe Lane was right. Maybe it was time to get to the bottom of it?

"Right. Later."

I hung up and finished my breakfast. The couple behind me

quietly paid their check and left. I swear I didn't hear them speak again. Sometimes it was fun to call people on their shit, even if I did it in a passive aggressive manner.

"Were they bothering you?" the server asked as I paid the check.

"Not really." I shrugged it off. Not many people would have understood, so I never talked about it to anyone other than Gabby and a few therapists I used to see.

"Well, have a great day. Thank you." She went to hand me my change and I waved her off.

"Thanks."

I remember wishing I had worn a hoodie, but it was too hot. Still, it would have been nice to have something to hide in as I ran home. There were more people out and more stares than before. I put on my headphones and did my best to ignore everyone.

By the time I returned, my mother's car was gone from the driveway. Not having to deal with her any more this morning was a great relief. I related to my father even less than I did my mother. He had stopped trying to awkwardly bridge the gap between us when I had hit puberty. Fortunately, I had not seen him at all. My parents didn't get along well. I knew better than to ask my mother about him.

After a shower, I turned the eating area into a workspace and unpacked my stuff. Lane had left several messages at that point. He was under a deadline and was determined to have me meet it, as well. He also apologized several times for our conversation in the club. I had most of the book finished, but a few pages needed something extra, and I could not determine what was missing. I sent him the drafts for input and to get him off my back. He would add the dialogue as soon as he got it.

With work done, I napped through lunch. It's how I like Bayview best, when I'm asleep. I did make sure to set an alarm in time to check on things before leaving to pick up Gabby. Vinnie joined me on the bed. His contented purr was enough to lull me to sleep this time.

Chapter Five

Gabby was waiting on the porch when I pulled into her mother's driveway. No one else was around. I didn't even see movement at the windows. My mother would have been peeking. I guessed Gabby's family was above that, or at least they were not as interested in what happened on their street as Ms. Evans was with ours.

"Hey. Did your day get any better?" she asked as she climbed in and shut the door.

"I don't know. I slept through most of it. I sent off a work in progress to Lane. He had a few ideas on how to make a couple things better. I was stuck on a few panels." I rubbed my right temple. There was residual pain there. It was always there. I often referred to it as my squatter. It was uninvited and unlikely to leave.

"Another graphic novel? I thought you hated those."

"I don't mind working with Lane. He's got some great ideas and he usually doesn't write about the spandex wearing testosterone filled assholes," I answered. It was true. Lane's books dealt less with machismo and more with adolescent issues. It was an area he handled very well. He had studied childhood education and psychology before going to art school.

"But since you sold that painting, I thought you didn't have to take those anymore. Can't you just concentrate on your painting?" she asked.

"I wish. I'm self-employed. It was a nice bump, and a lot went to starting a nest egg, but I have to pay insurance and taxes and all that other shit. It cleared a lot of bills out of the way and now I have savings." It was amazing how far a million dollars didn't go when you had to pay student loans, health care debt, taxes, commission, etc. There were times adulthood sucked. Having to explain why I wasn't rolling in money sucked more.

"My allergies are killing me," she complained. "The change in environment gets me every time." She pulled out a large, foul-smelling pill that looked more like a pellet of wood and put it in her mouth.

"Gross. Man, that stinks, whatever it is."

"That's the place." She pointed out the restaurant a block away and ignored my comment on her pill. "I hope they have veggie burgers. I'm hungry and I'd hate to drink on an empty stomach."

"I'm sure they do. Most places try to keep you people happy."

"You people?" She arched one brow. I had never been able to do that and had been secretly jealous of that for years. I had even gone so far as having my eyebrows waxed in an arch, but it didn't help. "You people?"

"I don't understand being a leaf eater, but hey, it suits you." I smiled and shook my head at her. "But burgers, man. They make life worth living." I loved a good burger as much as I loved my beloved candy bar. However, I never cooked them, and it was depressing to eat alone, so I rarely got to eat one since the times I did go out, I didn't do it to eat.

"Nice to know you appreciate something in life." She grinned at me. "Zu, Silas and Oliver will be here later, but I'd like to go ahead and get a table big enough for all of us."

"Yeah. That shouldn't be a problem." I looked around for the hostess. She ran forward as we approached. "Two to eat but three will join us in about an hour. Got room for us?"

"Do you mind sitting outside? Inside seating is reserved for the show tonight." She grabbed a couple of menus.

"Show?" Gabby asked.

"Yeah, it's a funk band. They're local. We have live music a few times a week."

"Outside is great," I told her. Visible through the window, the covered outside area, was filled with comfortable looking chairs around wrought-iron tables. It was also darker. "We've no problem with that."

"Then follow me." She led the way through a side door and out onto the patio. It was a nice space. "Here you go. Your server will be with you in a moment."

"Thank you." I took a seat against the railing so that I was looking at everyone and no one could sit behind me. I hated not seeing what was going on no matter where I was. Gabby sat down across the table.

"Sweet. It looks like their veggie burger is really vegan," she said happily. "I didn't know there would be a band. That okay?"

"Sounds fine to me. More people will be inside listening and not worrying about us." I leaned back in my chair and looked at the options. I admit to being a burger snob. "This looks promising. Not a lot of gimmicky burgers."

"You and burgers." She shook her head.

"I'm just glad you stopped hounding me about them," I told her after the server came to take our orders. We both got beers and fries, but drastically different burgers.

"I know a lost cause when I see one." She sighed and leaned back in her chair. Her fingers were drumming on the table. I knew she wanted a cigarette. That was her big sin, her drawback. We each had one according to Silas.

"Go ahead, smoke. It should be allowed out here." I looked around and spied an ashtray on the table beside us. With a disregard for gravity, I leaned my chair until I could snag the ashtray and pull it toward me.

"I didn't think you knew." She looked startled as I placed it before her.

"I could tell on the phone the other night. It's not a big deal, Gabs. Smoke. I don't judge."

"Yes, you do." She did the eyebrow thing again. "You hated my smoking when we were dating."

"True, but I don't judge you for it. Anymore anyway. Crutches help us walk, right?" I took a long gulp of beer wishing it was something stronger. That was my big sin, my drawback.

"Thanks." She reached in her pocket and pulled out a battered pack of cigarettes.

"You know, I hadn't noticed how expensive these things had become until I bought a pack the other day." I knew she alluded to the phone call telling her about Hawkins's death. She had revered him.

"I've not paid attention, really. You know I never smoked."

"Nope. You're a drinker."

"And I'm just a druggie, right?" a deep voice asked from just beyond the table. I almost choked on my beer.

"Silas?" It took me a moment to recognize him in the shadows. Once he's in the light, it's impossible to mistake him for anyone else. He had changed little. His brown hair was still impossibly curly and just barely touched with gray. His brown eyes twinkled with silent mischief I had never fully decoded.

"Claire. Gabby." He looked for a moment as if he wanted to hug us but settled with a nod and small wave. "I guess I'm early."

"Not terribly so." Gabby waved his observation away. "Come on. Take a seat."

"The other two miscreants on their way?" Silas eased himself into a chair. He grabbed a cigarette from the pack on the table and lit it.

"What? That's what you call us now? We don't have names?" I asked him, slightly annoyed but unsure why. He looked good. It looked as if the second trip through rehab had worked for him. He was wearing a bright orange flowered Hawaiian shirt that made my artistic temperament want to run and hide. The cargo shorts were expected after that. I forced myself to not check out his shoes.

"Fine. When are Oliver and Zu arriving?" He grabbed a coaster and spun it.

"Man, the dope really did kill brain cells, didn't it?" I scoffed. "She said everyone was supposed to meet at seven when she talked to you, didn't she?" The pain in my head spiked and then receded. "Sorry."

"Whatever, man." He flagged down our server. "Whatever you have on tap that's dark. Thanks."

"Not too picky, are you?" Gabby asked. "Never mind. When did you get in?"

"This morning." He leaned back and sighed. "Whoa. Check it out."

Silas drew our attention to a group that had just arrived. Several younger women walked onto the patio and settled around a large table. They were dressed in costumes, the one in the middle was wearing a crown.

"So, it's a group of kids." I glanced back at them. "Whoa."

For a moment, I saw Gwen. She was sitting not too far away with the other group, next to the young woman wearing the crown. It was the same heart-shaped face but aged a little. Then she shook her hair back and it was not Gwen after all. It was her sister. Which was a relief. The past few times I had seen Gwen, it had been a figment of my imagination, so I had been told.

"Fuck." Suddenly, I really didn't want to be there. I had made it a point, a priority, to avoid Gwen's family at all costs. I had done a fairly decent job. I had last seen them all at the memorial. I had even skipped Ms. Crosby's funeral.

"What?" Gabby turned around and then turned back so fast I'm surprised her head didn't fly off her shoulders. "Fuck. Last time I saw her she was running naked through the sprinklers in their backyard."

"You didn't go to the memorial service." I barely recognized my own voice. "It was brutal."

"That's Shelly?" Silas asked.

"Stephanie," I corrected. "Stephanie Crosby, Gwen's baby sister."

"Damn. If the hair was a little lighter." He shook his head. "Oliver's going to flip the fuck out."

"Don't tell me he's still saying he's in love with Gwen." It seemed ludicrous. I doubted they would have made it much beyond graduation.

"That's what the man says." Silas stopped as the server placed his beer in front of him. "Thanks. Plan to bring another round in five."

"Yes, sir." The server looked at us strangely but moved on to take orders from a different group.

"Anyway, he blames all his failed relationships on the one who literally got away."

"That's not funny." Gabby looked oddly serious. "We still don't, at least to my knowledge, have any fucking clue what happened. That doesn't give us the right to make jokes. I mean did you hear what happened to Gwen's family?" For all her bluster, Gabby was very tender hearted. It made her a damn good nurse and a much better friend than I probably deserved.

"Yes." I nodded. Silas didn't. "We'll tell you later, maybe."

"Good idea." He looked at the other table again. "Damn. She looks just like her. Poor kid."

"Is this where the party is?" I recognized Oliver's voice before I saw his face, which was strange since I had no memory of seeing him since Gwen's memorial. "What's up, family?"

"Not much, man." Silas stood up and they did that slap hand, half hug thing they have done since junior high.

"Oliver," I said, attempting to nod coolly. I really wished I had ordered something stronger. I made a promise to myself to order something like a sidecar or chaser or whatever with the next round. I felt anxiety fueled rage course through me. My self-control, which was never very good, slipped, and I didn't know why.

"Hi, Ollie." Gabby scooted to make room for him. He, of course, sat next to her, which put him across from me. Out of the other four, he was the one I got along with least, but again, I wasn't sure why. He just always made me feel slightly guilty.

"Gabby!" His voice was so loud the other tables looked at us. I could tell, by the weight of the stares and silence that we had been recognized. "Sorry."

"Jesus, Oliver. Just fucking announce we're here." I stood and made a lame excuse about beer to leave the table.

The band had not gone onstage yet, but the inside was crowded. Bar backs and servers were piling drinks and food on trays, weaving in and out of the crowd. All the tables and chairs had been pushed against the walls. The fearless stood for the shows, apparently.

I joined the short line for the bathroom. There were two of them and apparently both were unisex. That didn't bother me, nor did it seem to be an issue with the people waiting ahead of me. Soon, quicker than I expected, I was next and then done. I made sure my hair looked semi decent, lipstick not smeared, then I squared my shoulders and left the small bathroom.

"Claire?"

I turned, expecting to see another person I barely remembered or desperately wanted to forget. I certainly didn't recognize the voice.

"Yes?" My heart dropped as I looked up into eyes so like Gwen's in size and shape.

"Wow. You look great. Pretty much like how I remember you, only shorter." The woman laughed. "You don't recognize me, do you?"

"Um." I looked closely. I could not help it. They were so alike. I knew that face, but the colors were wrong. Dark, deep blue eyes though instead of light, almost ice blue ones. The hair was dark and short, not long and light brown. "Stephanie?"

"Yes." The woman laughed again. "I should have known you would have recognized me." She seemed happy to see me. I found that disturbing and a nice change.

"Wow. How are you?" It was disconcerting. Stephanie looked so much like Gwen I felt I was looking at a ghost or another hallucination. And then I kept expecting blows. "How's your dad?"

"He's good. Well, as good as can be expected. How are you? Did you come back just for this? The funeral?"

"Yes. Are you going? Were you in band?" I asked against my better judgment. My inner judge was screaming for a large screwdriver and a fast escape route.

"Bridgette's getting married tomorrow and tonight seemed like a good night for the party, but we didn't realize you guys would be here." She looked around. "I guess it makes sense. You all were pretty close to Mr. Hawkins."

"I guess we were." I felt raw. The conversation stung, and not all of it pleasantly.

"I'm glad you are." Stephanie embraced me. I had to stop myself from flinching. "It's so good to see you."

"You too." I almost lied. Gwen had been a hugger, as well. The younger woman smelled of something smoky with a touch of mint. It was nice and not overpowering.

"I'll let you get back to your friends." Stephanie released me. "Hopefully, I'll see you around. We can catch up."

"Yeah. Maybe," I told her. There was a part of me that still missed Gwen. That same part missed her family, as well. We had spent so much time with one another that it was like we were related. The aftermath of that loss and then the separation had not helped my state of mind at all. It had been so sudden and complete it had been like an emotional amputation. I still felt the nerve endings twitch.

"Long line?" Gabby asked as I returned to the table. Zubeida had completed the group.

"Yeah." I threw my napkin on top of my plate. I was done eating. "Hi, Zu."

She was wearing a crisp, white, short-sleeved shirt that looked amazing against her dark skin tone. I wanted to paint her portrait.

"Nice sale, congrats," she said. "My mom sent me a copy of the article. She was thrilled."

"Thank you. It's allowed me to buy a better brand of alcohol." I didn't want to discuss my success with them. In fact, I didn't want to discuss anything with them. At that moment, I was questioning my decision to leave my nice, comfortable apartment and drive hours away to a place I loved to avoid.

"I'm sure it has," Oliver said. "So, any idea what happened to the old man? I thought he was ageless."

"Cancer." I rolled my head and stretched the tension out of my neck and shoulders. Silas was dabbing away a nosebleed. "Any liquor stores open on this end of town?"

"Yeah, the one by the grocery store," Zu answered. She lived the closest to Bayview and visited her mother fairly often. I believe it was the casinos she visited more than her family, but I had no room to judge. "It closes at ten, I believe."

"Excellent." I had depleted my personal supply that afternoon. I looked up and caught Stephanie looking at us. She smiled briefly when she realized I caught her looking and turned back to her group. "What's the plan for tomorrow?"

"Antsy to leave?" Silas asked. His nosebleed seemed under control for the moment. I wondered about it before I remembered he once had a penchant for cocaine.

"Just moving the conversation along," I told him. The dull pounding in my head was back.

"It's a big deal. They're doing a memorial concert tomorrow afternoon at two and then the wake will be at Cobb's Funeral Home from five to eight. Funeral will be at the graveyard on the highway the day after," Gabby informed us.

"Figured the town would make it go on for two days," Oliver said, sneering. "Any excuse for a party here. Are we planning on going?"

"No," she answered. "But it might be a good idea."

"I didn't see that in the paper today. I checked at Mabel's at breakfast," I answered.

"So, are we going to the concert?" Silas asked.

"That's a lot of exposure," I reminded him. I didn't mind crowds unless I was in Bayview. It was easy to get lost in a crowd, at least other than there.

"I think we should," Zu said. "The chance for us to hang out and honor Hawkins should be taken."

"Me, too. Why the hell not? We'll meet there then." Oliver had gotten loud again. "Want to go bar hop, Si?"

"Sure." Silas shrugged. "Ladies?"

"No thanks," Zu declined. I shook my head and Gabby did, as well. I didn't know what their reasons for objecting to the outing was, but I knew mine. I was no stranger to the club scene, and I was well acquainted with the one-night stands that it often leads to. I declined because my head was pounding, and Stephanie kept cutting her eyes in our direction as if checking to see if we were still there. I didn't know what that meant, but it certainly did factor into my decision to go home instead of clubbing.

"See you tomorrow then." Oliver threw a bill on the table and waited for Silas to follow him to the parking lot.

"That was entertaining," I said before draining my beer. "You drive?"

"Yes. I'm staying at my parents, of course," Zu answered. "I had a free night at the casino, but I guess I wanted the full brutal treatment of being home."

"I hear ya." I waved our server down again. "Can we get the check, please?"

"Certainly." She hurried off to get it.

"Gabby, do you mind if we stop by the liquor store on the way to your place?" I asked as I got my wallet from my pocket.

"Here you go." The server was back quickly. I glanced at the bill and handed her my card. "Thank you."

"Hey, I can pay for my own, you know," Gabby protested.

"I know you can. You make more than I do," I answered. "I'm tired and my head aches and I'm not waiting for someone to do math and split the bill."

"Thank you," Zu said politely.

"No problem. So, we okay with the stop?" I asked.

"Yeah, it's not a problem," Gabby answered.

"I can take Gabby home. I'm closer." Zu stood up and pulled the keys from her purse.

"You sure?" Something compelled me to ask. It was fine with me. I sometimes felt a little condemnation from my friend when I would buy alcohol in her presence. She would usually go on a rant, and I just didn't feel like arguing with her.

"Yeah, not a problem."

"Thanks." It fit both situations that happened in that instant. The server handed me back the card and the receipt to sign and Gabby and Zu turned to leave.

I signed the paper and put up my card. I caught one final look at Stephanie before I turned and headed back to the street. I had not parked in the little parking area but on the street. Parallel parking was something I liked to do. Someone had once said it was a sign of insanity, but I didn't believe that. I had so many other signs.

The liquor store was where I remembered, and as Zu had stated, it was open. Mississippi laws stated that any alcohol stronger than beer had to be sold in certain, specially licensed stores. This one was nice. It had a large selection of wine and hard liquor. The woman behind the counter looked tired, too, and had glanced up only to make sure I didn't look underage. Between the crow's feet I never hid well and the streaks of gray, I felt comfortable that I looked older than the legal limit.

There were aisles and rows of bottles. I could feel the tension ease out of me. I found the vodka I usually purchased and then checked out the selection of whiskey. I usually carried a flask when I had the opportunity. It was currently empty sitting on the small kitchen counter unless Vinnie had knocked it off again. I had left it at home since we were meeting at a bar. It had felt redundant.

I had not been exaggerating to Zu and the others. Most of the money I had made from the sale of that painting had gone to make me debt free, which allowed me to use the money I made from freelance work for better quality alcohol. I splurged and bought the good stuff. I didn't know for certain how long I would be in Bayview and just how taxing the next few days would be, so I bought two bottles of each. Conveniently, they also had a cooler with soda and mixers in it. I picked up some orange juice and another flask, paid the lady and drove home.

Once back in the small apartment, I made myself a drink, refilled the old flask, washed the new plastic one and made sure Vinnie had food. I wasted a few minutes checking email and news sites as I finished the first one. By the time I had finished my second drink I was ready for bed. I curled around Vinnie and made a concentrated effort to fall asleep. For once, it worked.

Chapter Six

I was up at three in the morning after a few vivid dreams. I gave in to the inevitable and set up my easel and canvas. There was an image from one dream that was so clear it needed to be set in paint. That would happen a lot at night. I would sleep for some random amount of time and then spend the rest of the night lying in bed staring at the ceiling, drinking, painting, or doing anything other than sleeping.

I was usually a very methodical painter. It was the only time I planned anything. I would have something in mind, sketch it out and then outline it on canvas and paint in the color. I didn't do that this time. This one was more visceral. The image was burned into my brain so much that I saw it every time I closed my eyes. There was no need to sketch it first, anyway. It was almost as if I was tracing an image burned into my retinas.

I had sold a few paintings here and there. I had the freelance work and the graphic novel work with Lane. I even had a web comic that I started as therapy. It made a little money every month. I had planned it all out. I never painted halfcocked, except when I did one time. I painted by the seat of my pants and sold it for a small fortune. My friend, the gallery owner, told me I should have learned from that. Maybe I should have. Habits, though, are hard to break. I needed the routine, it was soothing.

By the time the sun was up, I had made a great start on it. I had been painting nonstop for two hours. I gave my hand and arm a break and went for a run. Besides, Mabel's not only had really good breakfast, but it was not my mother's kitchen. She tended toward healthy breakfast alternatives like yogurt and granola. At least Gabby would have been able to find something to eat there. However, I was a big fan of meat, eggs, and grease.

I wore a hat pulled low this time, feeling like a celebrity in hiding. No one bothered me. I was able to eat in peace, catching up on social media as I did so. Several of the people I socialized with in St. Louis had gone to a club and posted pictures. It was strange not to be in them. I skimmed through those posts and continued looking for anything that had to do with Bayview. I saw several memorial posts for Mr. Hawkins, but it didn't spark anything. I still didn't remember why I hated the man. I waited. Someone was bound to say something at the memorial concert. Something would jumpstart my memory, I was certain.

I turned my thoughts to the surprise that seeing Stephanie had been. I hallucinated, sort of, various times in my life. It had not been uncommon to see Gwen or something that reminded me of her. It usually lasted for a few seconds before I either blinked or it resolved itself into something else. I sighed and finished my coffee. I felt the need to be on the move again.

I ran back to the house and spent the rest of the morning painting. It put me in a better frame of mind. I had noticed that I didn't drink as much when I was working on a personal project. Painting has always been soothing for me. I drank, because that is one thing I did and did well, but I didn't do it in such quantities when I was painting.

My alarm went off, warning me it was time to shower and dress. I would not be picking Gabby up this afternoon. Her parents were going to the concert. She would ride with them. I declined to tease her about it. Navigating parent-child relationships as an adult was difficult enough, or so I had been told. It was a funny notion though. I laughed at the image of Gabby tucked into the backseat of her stepfather's car with her equally diminutive mother half turned to face her, speaking back and forth in rapid Spanish.

The school district had converted to a middle school-high school system rather than the junior-senior high program it had been when we had attended. The population had also tripled since then. The old high school was now the middle school, and the high school had a large brand-new building all to itself. I was relieved. There would be no ghosts in a building with no history.

The parking area was overflowing with many different vehicles, many had out of state plates. Mr. Hawkins had been the band director for more than thirty-five years. He had been a deacon in his church and was generally held in high regard by everyone. Everyone it seemed but me for some odd reason. Of course, I could not remember why that was. It was just a vague feeling of abject hatred tinged with incredible anger, seasoned with betrayal.

I walked slowly toward the doors after I found a space to park. Oliver was waiting outside. He looked somber in a dark suit. His blond hair was slicked back probably to hide that it was thinning. His face was as long and thin as it had been in high school, but his eyes and mouth were lined more than many guys our age. It looked as if he never smiled. I knew what that felt like.

"Guess the others aren't here yet," he said when I joined him.

"Looks like it." I leaned my back against the brick wall and kept my sunglasses on. "Wonder how many will be at the wake?"

"Beats me." He shrugged. "So, tell me about yourself, Claire. Something other than what they report around here. We have a few minutes to kill."

"Even a few minutes aren't worth it," I told him. "What about you?"

"Working at a little place called Wall Street." He grinned. "Making the dough."

"Really? Sweet." I knew he was lying. Oliver lied just to do it sometimes. I didn't have the energy to correct him. "I don't see a ring."

"Just haven't managed the married part yet." His smile faltered just a little. "What about you? Anybody waiting at home for you?"

"Just a cat." I almost felt ashamed phrasing it like that. Vinnie was so more than just a cat, but he was still not another human being. I realized then that we were all single. It had to be another symptom of whatever had scarred us. Then again, none of us had achieved our yearbook ambitions either.

"I had a cat in college. Not sure it was a good idea. The roommate took him when we graduated."

"There's Zu." I drew his attention away from himself. "And I think that's Silas back there."

"Looks like it. You know he can still party hard." Oliver laughed. "We didn't get back until early this morning. I thought about calling it long before, but I didn't want to leave my man high and dry."

"Glad you had fun." It was all I could think to say. Oliver and Silas both had been very intelligent guys in high school. They certainly didn't seem to have carried that into adulthood.

"Hi." Zu was immaculate in a black dress and heels. During the years she had allowed her hair to go natural. Her mother didn't approve. Ms. Okafor had embraced American culture. Zu had not discarded her Nigerian roots.

"You look nice," I told her.

"You do, as well. I wasn't sure you owned anything other than jeans." She caught herself. "Sorry. I'm a little nervous."

"Aren't we all?" I let it slide. I knew she was nervous and had temporarily forgotten that I had quit wearing jeans in high school. I was a lesbian, true, but not a denim flavored one. I smoothed the folds of my long, flowing skirt. Those had been my style since I had watched a foreign language film about an artist and copied her look the summer before our senior year.

"I'm not. What have we to be nervous about?" Oliver asked. "What's up, buddy?"

"I'm awake." Silas brushed the black mop of hair in futile attempt to get it to fall the same way. His dark eyes were slightly bloodshot, and his plain black suit wrinkled. "There's a lot of fucking people here."

"That there is," I agreed. I had nothing else to say. This type of crowd was a bit different from the type in which I usually lost myself.

"Where's Gabby?" Zu asked.

"She was riding with her mom and step-pop." I looked out across the crowd. "There she is."

Gabby was easy to spot. Her short, spiky raven black hair had blue highlights in the sun. She was wearing black slacks with a black shirt and a black sweater atop it, though it was not cold. Her parents walked a little behind her. At least her mother looked friendly.

"All together again," she said when she joined us. "Let's go find seats."

"Lead the way." No one wanted to lead. It was as if it would confirm us as a group.

People didn't seem to pay much attention to us when we were standing around outside. However, when we went inside the auditorium, heads turned to watch us pass. The whispers swelled like a buzz of angry bees. I had a hard time resisting the urge to smirk, wink or taunt them in some way. Instead, I stared straight ahead and followed Gabby to a row that had five empty seats. They already thought we were crazy. Starting a scene here wouldn't be a good idea. Besides, we were vastly outnumbered and I wasn't sure I could count on any of my friends to back me up.

"Man, sometimes I really don't miss being here," she muttered as we took our seats.

"Me either."

"You know, it probably wouldn't be so bad if we were seen more," Silas suggested.

"I'm a fucking person, not an object of curiosity." I didn't take the trouble to keep my voice down. "I mean, what? No one has ever done anything around here worth talking about in twenty years?" It bothered me we were still considered newsworthy after so long. Anytime one of us did something like graduate or get promoted or whatever, it got a write up in the paper.

"I think one of the local preachers ran off with a married woman he was counseling," Zu said. "It's still a small community. Not much happens here."

"Bullshit." I was not having it. My head was starting to hurt. I looked and noticed Silas was dabbing at a nosebleed again. "You get those often?"

"Yeah. You?" he asked.

"No. Headaches." It was as close as we had come to discussing anything since we had left Bayview as far as I could remember. I looked to Gabby. "How are your ears?"

"My ears are fine. Why wouldn't they be? You okay? You seem nervous," Gabby said. "Looks like they're about to start."

"Good. We can't see the stares when the lights are out," I muttered. Silas chuckled.

There was movement on the stage. The curtain was closed, the school's insignia prominently displayed. The house lights went dim and a bright spotlight hit the area where the curtains split. A tall, balding man in an ill fitted, shiny suit approached the microphone. His mustache was epic at least.

"Ladies and gentlemen. Students. Thank you for attending. For those of you who do not know me, I'm Reggie Clark. I have the honor of being the principal here." There was a small round of applause. "I had the pleasure of working with Mr. Hawkins when he was our band director. He was a good man and will be greatly missed." The applause was longer and louder this time. "So, without taking up too much of your time, we have a memorial concert planned. Our band program is one of the best in the state. For your enjoyment and to give music to our grief, each level of students will be performing. There will be a short break between each so we can get the students situated. We start here with the elementary students. I'll let them take the stage. Thank you."

We soon discovered that the principal had not been kidding. He had said every band and that is what we got. I made it through the beginner band without going crazy. They fell apart twice, but the director was good enough to get them back righted. The intermediate band was almost as bad. This group was filled with second year musicians. They had survived beginning band but were still new to the whole thing. It was not until the break before the third band that I decided I needed air. I needed air and whisky. I needed lots of both.

I excused myself and walked outside. A few others had the same idea. There were the usual smokers and parents on cell phones. A group of teenagers who were too cool to be inside all the time were outside, as well. I walked off a little way, leaned against the warm brick and pulled out my flask.

"It's not even five o'clock yet." I heard the comment from the crowd, but I could not see who made it.

"Leave her alone. She probably needs to drink after what they did." A man's voice, but again I could not see who said anything.

"You get that a lot?" I was so busy looking at the crowd, trying to identify the speakers, that I didn't realize Stephanie had walked up to me.

"Only when I'm here," I answered. I took another pull off the flask before closing it and putting it back in my pocket. All I could do now is wait for the warmth to settle in my belly and the tension to drain a little from my shoulders. "I don't get it. It's not like we have matching t-shirts or anything."

"That must be terrible. No wonder you guys hardly ever come home," she said sympathetically.

"Yeah, well, you never get used to it." I shrugged it off. "Thought you had a wedding or something." She was not quite dressed for a wedding. She was wearing a pair of dark khakis, a crisp dress shirt tucked in with the sleeves rolled up, sneakers and mirrored sunglasses. I did tend to like them a little butch. I felt just the tiniest flutter of attraction.

"I do actually. It's just not until later. My little cousin is in the jazz band, so I came to see the performance." She explained. "I was wondering if you would like to meet for coffee or something tomorrow."

"Um." It caught me off guard. "I don't mean to be rude, but why?"

All I could see was my own reflection, and it didn't tell me much about what the woman behind those sunglasses was thinking. All I learned was my hair was a little windswept and my green eyes were slightly bloodshot.

"Because you were my sister's best friend. You were almost like an older sister to me, too." Stephanie shrugged. "I just thought it would be nice to catch up."

"Well." I fully intended to decline. In fact, I started to say the correct words and then my mouth betrayed me. "Sure. When and where?"

"Great." She smiled a not-quite-Gwen's smile. This one was a little crooked and showed a mouth of straight, white teeth. "Mabel's is the place for coffee still. Do you want to meet before the funeral or after?"

"Before. If you're free I've been going for a run and then eating breakfast at Mabel's in the morning. We can meet then." I had agreed to meet, but I was set on dictating the terms.

"Excellent. What time? Six thirty?" Whether or not she knew it, she had called my bluff. I had hoped that would have been too early or too inconvenient a time for her.

"Usually around then." I said it like I've been doing it for years instead of two days.

"Okay. I'll see you tomorrow morning then." She smiled and then gestured back at the building. "I guess we should go back in."

"Yeah. I guess so." I sighed and pushed myself off the wall. I didn't wait for her but went back in and sat back down between Gabby and Silas. I felt raw. Every interaction with strangers was like sandpaper on my skin.

"What's going on?" Gabby asked. She was holding her wrist like she was taking her pulse.

"Nothing. Just needed some fresh air," I told her. I still didn't feel the warmth from the drink. It irritated me. "What do you know about Stephanie Crosby?"

"Not much." She shrugged. "Why?" She pulled something from her purse. I looked away. I didn't want to see whatever it was.

"She wants to meet for coffee," I said slowly. It was still boggling my mind.

"Wow. Okay." Gabby looked a little shocked. "Maybe she thinks you're cute?"

"Doubtful." I slid down in my chair a little. Already I was regretting agreeing to meet.

"You never know. She's kinda hot." Silas joined our conversation after he returned to his seat. His eyes were a little dilated. "Damn though, she looks like Gwen, don't you think so, Claire?"

"Can we not mention her here?" For some odd reason it upset me to hear Silas say her name. "For fuck's sake."

Out of the corner of my eye, I saw Gabby's jaw tighten at my outburst. It made me feel vaguely guilty until I caught a whiff of the horrible hand sanitizer she favored. Gabby's fear of germs was wreaking havoc on my sinuses. The longer she worked at the ER, the worse it got.

"Hey, keep it down." He shushed me. "We don't want them to pay attention to us anymore than they already are."

"Yeah, whatever." If there had ever been a time when an entire area needed amnesia, I felt that was it.

"Look, I was wondering if you guys wanted to hang next weekend?" he asked.

"We'll talk about it later." I waved him off as the houselights fell again.

After the next group of kids playing spirituals and old standards, apparently those were some of Mr. Hawkins's favorite types of music, performed, we were passing my flask back and forth. Even Zu and Gabby were taking hits off it, despite the nurse's fear of germs. It almost made things bearable.

"We've got an hour and half before the wake. Want to grab something to eat?" Oliver asked as the lights came back on and people started leaving. He looked as if he rarely ate a decent meal. I was sure he would tell us otherwise.

"There's a decent Mexican restaurant between here and there," Zu said.

"I guess." I looked around at the others. Like it or not, we were a group. "Fine. I'll meet you there." I needed a break from people, and I needed control of my car stereo.

As they decided who would ride with whom, I walked outside and to my car. Though I had been drinking, I was far from drunk. I turned on something soothing and sat in my car for a long minute. When the traffic had thinned enough, I drove to the restaurant Zu had suggested. I almost wish I had not. Part of me wanted to just say the hell with it and drive straight back to St. Louis, stopping only long enough to pick up Vinnie and my painting in progress.

Chapter Seven

I had never eaten at that Mexican restaurant before then. It seemed like any other locally owned place. There were TVs with sports around the walls, local art and a mixture of booths and wobbly tables. I was the first to arrive, so I had the hostess lead me to a table for five. Ominously, the table was a six person one. My head hurt.

"Hey. Did you get queso?" Silas asked as he took the seat opposite.

"I haven't ordered anything," I answered. "Just you?"

"So far. I think Gabby and Zu rode together. Oliver's on his motorcycle."

"Why are we here, Silas?" I could not resist asking. I had always enjoyed talking to him, or so I remembered. We had had some strange, in-depth conversations while stoned in high school. I was the artistic liberal and he was the fiscal conservative. It made for some entertaining discussions.

"Here now? To eat." He looked at the menu. "Here on earth? Beats the hell out of me. Here in Bayview? You know, I don't know."

"I feel like that should bother us more, but when I try to think about it, I get a fucking miserable headache." I could feel one forming then. "The alcohol helps."

"The pot helps. You off the other meds? Never mind. It's not any of my business. I stopped everything else, though. It was too late to stop the inner nose damage. Of course, I've only been out of rehab this time for a few months." He wiped the blood that was falling from his nose away. "The others here?"

"Yeah." I watched them walk in and look around. "Just got here."

Once everyone was seated, the server brought us all glasses of water, two baskets of tortilla chips and salsa. We ordered food and drink. It was happy hour. I was thrilled. I felt as if I could stomach a few margaritas. I would have gone with straight tequila, but I didn't feel like going to jail for murder or rampant nudity.

"Anyone learn anything?" Oliver asked as the server left to put in our order.

"Not really." I rubbed my right temple. Sometimes it felt as if I could rub the pain away if I pressed hard enough.

"Well, let's get reacquainted." Zu folded her napkin in her lap and looked around at us all. "I'm not sure who has kept up with whom. I for one would like to know more about what happened to my friends. Something other than the highlights from the paper or the rumors my mom tells me about."

"Me, too," I said at the same time as Silas. The sarcasm I used was heavy. I could have named us easily, based on the limited amount I knew of them. Alcoholic, compulsive gambler, hypochondriac, drug addict, and pathological liar. Claire, Zu, Gabby, Silas and Oliver.

"Excellent." Oliver looked excited. "I'll go first. I tend bar. I'm not married, and I have a decent saltwater fish tank."

"I'm not married either," Zu said. "I do have a guy I've been seeing pretty regularly for a few years. We've been talking about moving in together, but I'm not sure about it. I'm a junior associate at a large law firm. Well, I haven't made partner, but it's not easy to do that and be a Black woman, at least not in New Orleans."

"I'm single and an emergency room nurse." Gabby waved her left hand in the air as if underscoring the lack of a ring. "Silas, you next?"

"Single. I do as little as possible," Silas answered. We laughed. "I've traveled. Mostly though I do a few meetings and emails for my dad." We understood. Silas's family was very wealthy. He obviously worked for them in some capacity.

"Commercial artist. Very single," I told them. It was funny how we didn't state the real people we were. "Seems to be a common thread." It was easy to hide behind titles and professions.

"But you've been a little successful at least," Oliver pointed out. "I mean apparently you sold a painting for a lot. My mom told me. And Silas works for his dad and makes a ton."

"Yeah, but I'm just staying afloat with everything else," I corrected him. "And before that I was swimming in debt." Even with insurance, mental health care was expensive.

"I get paid a lot of money not to do much," Silas said. "I don't consider that success."

"My mom has our senior yearbook at her house, prominently displayed on a shelf. I looked at it last night." Gabby leaned forward. "We all wanted so much more from life than we're getting. We had dreams and ambitions"

"Isn't that normal?" Oliver asked. "Excellent. Thanks," he said when the server placed our drinks in front of us. My margarita was large, blue, and had an umbrella. As long as it contained alcohol, I was okay with that.

"Fuck." The TV nearest us stopped playing and went to static and feedback. All five of us jumped and put our hands over our ears.

"That was odd." Silas stated mildly when someone took pity on us and changed the channel.

"I thought it was just me." I was amazed. They had problems with it, too. I wondered if they heard things too or saw things like I did. I didn't want to ask, though. The specter of madness is hard to leave behind. I'd worked hard to make sure mine was still well hidden.

"No. Not just you." Oliver's voice was oddly detached. He kept looking in that direction. I wish I knew what he was looking at or looking for.

"Let's just eat and get out of here." Gabby was rubbing her ears. "We still need to go to that wake."

"Agreed." Silas sighed.

The meal was delivered not long after the drinks arrived. We kept the conversation light after that. I could not tell if the static had just happened or if the universe was trying to keep us from talking about that disastrous boat trip. It was feeling as if we needed to talk about it though and that scared me. It scared the hell out of me. The few times I had tried to remember anything, it had not gone well at all.

We paid the check and left in the same groups in which we had arrived. Cobb's Funeral Home was downtown and within good walking distance to my house. By the time we got there, Silas in the lead and Oliver bringing up the rear, the parking lot was packed. We ended up parking down the street and walking a block.

"Whoa." Silas pointed at the building as we approached.

"Wow." If the parking lot had been a surprise, it was nothing to the line of people waiting to pay their respects, which was out the door. "This is going to take all night."

"We got nothing else to do." Oliver straightened his tie. "Let's show them who they've been talking about for all these years."

It was not as awesome as he made it sound. In real life, there was no slow-motion pan as we walked past bug-eyed stares with a light breeze artfully tousling our hair. We walked up to the building, found the end of the line, and stood there. It took two hours before we reached the door. Mr. Hawkins knew a lot of people. We recognized some of them. Some people seemed to have recognized us. No one spoke to us though. We stayed in our little group, isolated by a decades old event we could not remember.

"What's this?" Gabby asked after an usher handed her a card with Mr. Hawkins's picture on it.

"Memorial card," Zu answered. "If you're Catholic, it's a prayer card."

"Cards against death," Silas muttered, turning his. "He got old."

"Yes, he did." I looked down at mine. A black-and-white image of Mr. Robert Hawkins was staring up at me above thick glasses. I shivered.

It was just a flash of something. I didn't know what, but for a moment I was standing in the band hall. I could smell sweat, grease, and the slightly metallic scent I associated with it. I could hear voices. Two people were talking. I think I was one of them. I couldn't tell. The fog that lives in my head was denser than normal.

"Claire?" Gabby had her arm around my waist and one hand on my neck. "Don't pass out. Breathe."

"What? I wasn't going to pass out," I said weakly. Silas was urgently trying to hand me a bottle of water and Zu had a little paper fan going. Oliver was standing around, glaring at everyone with the memorial card balled up in his fist.

"You sure? You went stiff as a board and your eyes glazed." Gabby slowly removed her hands. "Now you're clammy. What the fuck, Claire?"

"I don't know. I just looked at the picture." I was aware of people staring at me.

"I tried not to." Silas held his up. He had folded it, hiding the picture on the inside of the fold. "He's in there, isn't he?"

"Seems to be, otherwise this would be kind of a waste." My throat felt dry. It was difficult to get the words out. My head didn't hurt precisely, but the world wanted to spin the opposite direction and the tacos we had eaten for dinner wanted to make a reappearance.

"Are you okay?" Gabby asked again. She appeared concerned. The people around us in line were doing their best to pretend they were ignoring us after Oliver puffed his chest out and stared them down. I was going to live. Their interest waned as a result.

"Yeah." I waved her off and took a long drink of water. "Not sure what happened, but I'm okay."

"We're moving." Oliver indicated the gap between our group and the one in front of us.

Once we got beyond the doors by several feet, the line moved faster. We found out why as we entered the actual funeral room with the coffin. Several people were sitting on pews or standing around in groups along the walkways. There were a lot of teenagers there. I assumed they were his students. Then again, they could have been there with their parents, but I doubted that somehow. Mr. Hawkins had directed the band even when undergoing his first chemo treatments. From what my mother had said, he only retired when he simply couldn't do it anymore. That had only been a year prior.

I noticed a group of teenagers, seniors by the look of them, standing in the back corner of the room. It was eerie how much they reminded me of my friends at that age. It could have been us, or maybe they could become us. It was like looking in a distorted mirror, the perception a bit fish eyed.

"I can't believe you all made it." Sylvia Hawkins had been everyone's mother in band. "Robert would have been so happy."

"We're sorry for your loss," Oliver said. "He was a great man."

My voice was useless. I kept staring at the coffin and the man lying inside it. It was definitely him. They had put his glasses on him. His beard looked neat and combed. Thinning red hair was parted on the left and smoothed to the right to deemphasize a high forehead. He looked like he was made of wax. The flowers covered up most of it, but there was still a faint hint of formaldehyde.

"I know you are, sweetie." She patted him on the arm. "Robert always wanted to keep up with you five. He was so devastated after what happened to Gwen that he almost retired, but he kept on. At least he went in his sleep."

"You seem at peace with it," Gabby observed.

"Not at all." She laughed. People turned to look, and she covered her mouth with her hand. "It's like waves. One minute I'm frozen, crushed and can't do anything. The next one comes, and I've got energy to rearrange the house."

"It must be difficult." Silas's voice was constricted. He looked as if he was about to vomit or run out the nearest exit. Probably both.

"It is. Thank you all for coming. You'll have to come to the house one day, after the funeral tomorrow. A lot of people will be coming back to our house. Y'all should come, too. He would have liked that." Her brown eyes were tired. The bags under them were enormous. Her hair was trying to escape from the severe bun she normally wore. She looked old, sad and vulnerable.

"Thank you." I was not sure the sound came out of my mouth, but I knew it formed the words.

There was a lot of whispering as we walked back up the aisle and outside. Night had truly fallen. The quarter moon was low hanging and orange. It looked like his smile, no lips and smoke-stained teeth.

"I guess this is all for tonight?" Zu asked as we walked back to our cars. She sounded tired.

"I think we need to talk about what happened. I think it's time we tried to remember." Gabby stopped in the middle of the street and blocked our way. "Seriously guys. There's so much we don't remember."

"What do you think we ought to do?" I asked her. "I've tried to remember. I've tried hypnosis and meditating and everything thing else I could think of. The only things I've gotten from it are fucking brutal headaches, an inability to sleep without lots of alcoholic help and crazy fucking dreams when I can sleep."

"That's pretty much me, too," Silas admitted. "I have to get high just to relax enough to attempt sleep. I get nosebleeds constantly and no one can figure out why. No one. I've been in therapy. I've been to rehab. I've traveled to Nepal. I've done the whole enlightenment thing. There's nothing. Those three days do not exist."

"Look, I want to know what happened to Gwen as much as you do, maybe more, but maybe it's best if we all finally put it behind us." Oliver spread his hands out in front of him as if pleading with us.

"Really, Ollie?" Zu rounded on him. "Wouldn't you like to know just what happened to your high school sweetheart since you've always maintained that you didn't do it."

"You should know better than to argue with a lawyer, Oliver." Silas patted him on the back. "I'm game. Let's figure out what we can do. Where can we do this?"

"Can we at least wait until after the funeral?" Oliver asked. "I mean we're not going anywhere, right?"

"I don't know. Are you? I'm not. I got a week's paid vacation to come down here. I'm not leaving until it's through," Gabby promised. "What about you, Claire?"

"Shit." I sighed. "I can stay until whenever. Most of my work stuff is with me. I guess it's a good thing no one could watch Vinnie after all." I didn't want to stay, not really, but on the other hand, for once I wanted answers.

"All right. Tomorrow, after the funeral, we'll find someplace quiet and not full of strangers and talk," Gabby said.

"With lots of alcohol," Silas said. "We'll need it, I'm sure."

"Do you need a ride back to your parents?" I asked Gabby.

"Yeah, if you don't mind."

"Good. I wasn't going straight home," Zu admitted. I assumed she was heading for a casino. I imagined the lights and sounds were soothing, it was the thought of losing money that kept me away from them.

"See you tomorrow," Oliver called as he pulled on his motorcycle helmet.

"Later." I raised my hand in a wave.

"So, what happened when you saw the body?" Gabby asked as soon as we were in the car.

"Nothing. Why? Did something happen to you? Did you see something?" I asked.

"Why would you ask if I saw something?"

"Did you?" I didn't elaborate.

"No. You did though, when you almost passed out, didn't you?" She rolled the window down and pulled out a cigarette. "What the fuck, Claire?"

"I don't know. I saw or rather heard two people talking, but I don't know what they were saying. I think it was in the band hall."

"Do you know why I work in an emergency room?" Her question threw me, but she didn't wait for an answer. "Because it's usually loud and bright. There's always something going on and I dig that. I need that stress to function at my best. I thrive on it. You though, I don't get it. I mean." She breathed out audibly. "A lot of people come through my ER in Memphis. It's only calm occasionally. I don't really like quiet. I don't know how you do it."

"I always have music playing unless I'm in the car then it's an audio book. I'm not fond of silence either. I just hate flipping channels and stations, you know." Even in a crowd, silence bothered me. I wanted to be always surrounded by noise. My mind didn't like the quiet. It gave it too much time to think and to remember.

"I know. I won't watch TV. Every time I go into our break room, I turn the TV off. It's all news and trash."

"You gonna light that cigarette?" I asked. She kept tapping it on her lighter.

"No. Just holding it is soothing."

"Think you'll quit again?"

"Are you dosing yourself? You've been drinking a lot more than normal." Her tone was gentle. It could have been so much harsher. Maybe it should have been.

"No. Of course not." I lied easily.

"Of course not." I glanced to see that she was looking out the window. "Would you mind terribly driving through somewhere and getting a soymilk latte? My sugar is dropping."

"I don't mind at all." Believe it or not, I didn't mind. I had not had a proper drink in a few hours, since the restaurant, but I felt mellower, less prickly than I normally would have. I was not sure how long it would last, but I figured I had at least long enough to get my friend a latte and get her home safely. It really did go that long, but no longer. It took several shots of the vodka I had stashed in the freezer before I could face even the idea of sleep.

Chapter Eight

I had forgotten my agreement with Stephanie until I entered Mabel's the next morning. After I had dropped Gabby off at her parents' house, I had made it back to mine before the anxiety bubbled back to the surface. I had spent a few hours painting, a couple making the changes Lane had suggested to the backgrounds and drinking.

My sleep that night had been scant and poor. I had dreamed every time I closed my eyes it seemed, but I was awake again not long after. I had memory dreams, I had crazy dreams, and everything in between. Finally, as the sun rose, I gave up and went for my morning run.

I ran farther than I had the past few days, down to the beach and around by the pier. It was my first good run since returning to Bayview. As a result, when I entered Mabel's, I claimed a booth. It felt good to stretch my legs out under the table and use the bottom of the seat across to flex my calves. They felt tight after running so long. I had just gone through the menu, looking for something other than eggs, ham and toast, when Stephanie arrived.

"Good morning." She looked very chipper, and it was irrationally annoying. "Did you have a good run?"

"Yeah." I shrugged.

"Which is it?"

"What?" I was confused. She slid into the booth opposite, and I had to move my legs.

"You shrugged but said yeah. So? Did you have a good run or was it meh?" she asked. She seemed a bit amused by it. I tried not to be very resentful. I hated people who got a full night's sleep and always seemed restful. It was unnatural.

"It was fine." I looked her in the eyes. I wanted to see if she would lie about something. "You're not a reporter, are you?"

"No," she answered once she stopped laughing. "Not even close. I'm a chef. I have a catering business and a restaurant I own downtown."

"That's great." I was in this now. I was tired and hungry, but also curious. "Is that something you've always wanted to do?"

"Yes. It's not what my mother wanted me to do, but…" She shrugged. "My dad was okay with it. What about you? You recently sold some art, didn't you? There was a write up in the paper about it."

"I sold a painting." I felt a little humble for some reason. Maybe it was the curious look in those almond shaped eyes. "I've sold a few here and there. Mostly I do freelance commercial work."

"Like advertising?" I had a hard time looking her in those eyes. My mind wanted to see her sister. I had micro breaks with reality every time I looked at her.

"Not exactly. I do some actual art and some artwork." I normally hated telling people what I did. "I do a lot of art for graphic novels and stuff. A friend of mine from art school writes this crazy series and I do his art. It's not a huge series though, not one of the big ones. Independent."

"Really? Which series?" She looked genuinely interested.

"*Robin Blind.*" Maybe it was because she looked so much like her sister that I told her. I never tell anyone. I was not necessarily ashamed of it, but somehow perceived I was failing to live up to someone's expectations.

"Holy shit. You're Ursula McAdams? I mean, I figured that was a pen name, but damn. Really?" She looked impressed.

"Yeah." It startled me. I had never met anyone who knew our work before. I had done the question-and-answer sessions on various websites, but I had never met a fan in real life. It added to the surrealness of the meeting.

"So, you do that web series then, right? *The Acorn in the Bayou?*" She leaned across the table and put her head on her hands. That slightly crooked smile was back, and it lit up her eyes. My mouth went dry.

"I do that, as well." It felt good to admit it. No one knew. Gabby and Lane knew, but no one else. No one really seemed interested enough to ask just what it was that I drew. Could be my fault, maybe people were interested, and I just didn't know. I doubted that though.

"Man, I read that every day. Or every day it's updated anyway. I've got your graphic novels, too. I had no idea."

"Really?" All at once she's not Gwen and I have no trouble looking at her and seeing anyone but Stephanie. Gwen had not been a fan of science fiction or art. I had no memories of a supportive Gwen. In fact, I had found it shocking how suddenly I was able to tell them apart with ease. Whatever happened, whatever she had said, or I had felt, had killed the ghost of Gwen from trying to possess my impression of her sister, Stephanie.

"Really." She paused for a moment. "They're kinda giving us space. Do you want to order?"

"I'm starving and I could really use a cup of coffee." I had not done more than glance at the menu. My head was pounding, and my vision was blurry around the edges. I needed caffeine in the worst way.

The same server I had seen for the past few days came and took our order. I just asked for the special and coffee. Stephanie did the same. The server did look at us oddly as she took our order. I guess she had figured out who the players were.

"Did you enjoy the concert?" I asked. I was eager to move the conversation away from myself.

"I did. I'll admit it was a little jarring to listen to the first couple of performances, though." She fiddled with the saltshaker.

"They're beginners. Not everyone can play beautifully out of the gate."

"I was never in band. Neither was Dylan. Dad wouldn't allow it."

"Why?" That was strange to me. It certainly set off alarm bells since he supported Gwen in band. If the younger kids had not been allowed to participate in something as benign as band, had their father suspected something foul with Hawkins? Had he blamed him? I had questions about her questions and the poor man was not even in reach for me to pester.

"I don't know exactly. It's not like he kept us from doing everything Gwen did. I mean, we could breathe and go to school and all, but some things he just would not budge on." The bowl of creamers had replaced the saltshaker as the focus of her fidgeting. She had long fingers with short, well-kept nails. Her hands were graceful and expressive. I struggled to pull my mind from the gutter.

"Would you have been in band if given the chance?" I asked. I watched, fascinated, as she built a little tower out of the creamers.

"Probably not. I have no sense of rhythm and I can't tell one note from another." She smirked a little when she said that. It made one side of her mouth go slightly higher than the other. It was endearing.

"That would definitely be a setback if you had dreams of being the next big jazz musician," I said drolly. Our coffee arrived. Just the smell of it seemed to embrace my soul. "So, what is Dylan up to these days?" I had not seen her brother since the memorial.

"He's a cop," she said as I snagged the top creamer for my coffee.

"Really?" I almost spilled both the creamer and my coffee. "Hot! Shit." I grabbed a napkin and wiped the small puddle of hotter than expected coffee. The tip of my tongue felt permanently damaged.

"I bet it is." She quirked an eyebrow at me but said nothing. "He's not here. He moved to Gilbert County after college. He's a sheriff's deputy out there."

"Good for him. He always was a little snitch." I laughed. It was easy to remember the times Dylan would run squealing to his mother about something Gwen or I had said or done. "Always about rules."

"Yeah, he still is." She smiled, too. "You mind if I tell you something, honestly?"

"Um." I sensed danger of the emotional variety. "Okay."

"I missed you, too. I mean." She brushed her bangs away from her face. Her hair was just long enough to have bangs, or at least a section that tended to fall into her eyes. "You and Gwen were always together. It's almost as if I lost two sisters when she left us."

"Oh." I had nothing to say to that. How was I to explain the pain and guilt I had felt? That I still felt?

"I don't want to make you feel bad. I just kinda felt like I needed to tell you." She shrugged her shoulders a little and looked off toward the door. The tower of creamer toppled and fell. I placed them back in the bowl, giving me something to do other than look at her.

"I understand." It was as much as I could admit. "It must have been rough after your mom passed." I didn't dwell on it as it had hurt me, too. I didn't want to imagine Stephanie's pain.

"Yeah." For the first time I heard bitterness. "People always ask how it was when we lost mom. I swear I want to tell them she wasn't lost. I know exactly where she is and she's the one who put herself there."

"You don't talk about this often, do you?" I could almost hear the pent-up frustration and anger in her voice. To have her mother die suddenly two years after Gwen disappeared must have been debilitating.

"No." She put both hands around her coffee mug to steady herself. "I'm sorry. I don't know why I said that. I just feel as if I can talk to you, and you won't judge."

"Are you kidding?" I scoffed. "I'm one of the most judgmental people you'll ever meet."

"I don't think you are. You have a seriously harsh façade though. I guess after everything that's happened, you need it. It can't be easy, always in the public mind here."

"Maybe." I waited for the question, but it never came. Our food did, however. "Man, I'm starving."

"Me, too." I watched out of the corner of my eyes as Stephanie added salt and pepper to her eggs. Strangely, I felt comfortable. It was almost as if I had made a friend. I had not felt that in a very long time.

I could not tell if it was the ghost of Gwen or something uniquely Stephanie.

"What are you doing after the funeral today?" she asked.

"Dinner with the guys I think." For such an innocent question, it filled me with dread. My good feeling was slowly evaporating. "Nothing special."

"How long are you in town for?"

"Did you have Ms. Nesbit?" I asked. I was desperate for a distraction.

"I did. Why?" She looked at me curiously.

"She would have um, failed you for that dangling participle."

"Probably. I'm a chef though. My grammar doesn't have to be perfect." She smiled that quirky grin again. Shit. I could sense trouble ahead. "I was just wondering if maybe, if you had time, you'd want to come checkout the restaurant."

"Yeah, I think I would." I could not help myself and smiled back.

"Excellent." She pulled out a bill and a card from her wallet. "This is for breakfast. And this is for you to call me. It's got the cell and the kitchen number on there."

"Thanks, but I can pay for my share," I protested. I was unaccustomed to such chivalry. It was kind of nice.

"I know you can." She stood. "Thanks for meeting me for breakfast." She winked, and then she was gone.

"Fuck." I watched her walk out the door. I was in trouble. I rubbed my face. My hands trembled. How could I find her sexually attractive? It wasn't right.

Chapter Nine

"You ever wonder why Hawkins was interested in us after we left school?" Gabby asked as we parked at the cemetery. Zu had picked her up and the two of them had fetched me at my house. It seemed easier that way. I had been drinking too much to trust myself behind the wheel.

"We'll talk about it later," Zu said. She had seemed on edge since the moment we had gotten in the car.

I could not blame her. We were all on edge. I, at least, had gotten little sleep. After breakfast, I had returned home with the idea that I would continue working. I had not. In fact, I am not sure what I did other than sit on the bed, drink, and pet Vinnie. It was not until Gabby called that I rejoined the day. That had been scary enough. Zu's attitude and Gabby's sudden need for constant conversation just compounded my anxiety. I was tipping back the flask before we had made it to the corner.

Mr. Hawkins had chosen a graveside service, or someone had chosen for him. When we approached where the awning was, it was clear that we would not be close enough to hear the service. That was fine with me. We stayed in the back. Silas and Oliver joined us there and remained respectfully silent. That was difficult to do as people kept turning around to look at us. A few of them snapped pictures of us with their cell phones.

The worst part was we were not far from Gwen's grave. It was empty, but it had a headstone. Her mother occupied the space next to it, eternally waiting for her daughter to come home. I felt the sting of tears and pushed them down. I would not cry and have people misinterpret it as mourning for Hawkins.

After about twenty minutes, there was movement along the edges of the crowd and people headed to their cars. Some stayed and milled around in little groups. Some of them kept glancing our way. A few took hesitant steps in our direction and then stopped. I ignored them.

"What now?" I asked the group. "Do we want to go to the house?"

"I don't know." Silas stopped what he was saying and addressed the newcomers. "Can we help you?"

"You don't remember me, do you?" A woman about our age stood in front of us. Her dark hair was streaked with gray. Her eyes were so bloodshot I could not tell what color they were. She started loud and went to shrieking. "I'm Twyla. Gwen and I were best friends and you bastards killed her. Couldn't stand staying out there so you left her, huh?"

"What?" Oliver paled. "No."

"You weren't Gwen's best friend," I told her. It was an automatic response. My head started pounding and the horizon tilted just a little. "Who are you, even?" There was a strange buzzing in my ears. Having everyone stare at us, at me, made me nauseous.

"I remember you." Silas looked over his sunglasses. "You're that special ed freak. You kept telling everyone you were dating Sean, the basketball captain. And you made up all those lies about Coach O'Bryan. You cost an innocent man his job."

"I did no such thing." She really was practically yelling. Her voice hurt my ears. It was shrill and quavering. We were attracting a crowd. "You left her. She was pure and awesome and you left her. Savages."

"We didn't kill anyone." Gabby spoke softly and stepped forward. She held her hands out in front of her with her palms facing the sky. She was the only one of us who knew how to deal with real crazy from a professional standpoint. "It's okay. I understand why you would think so. There's a lot of mystery there. Most of it we don't know. But I promise you, we didn't kill anyone."

"Liar!" Twyla screamed, twitched a little to the side, and then made the tiniest lunge. "She doesn't like you anyway."

I have heard that sometimes time slows down, that some people have the ability to see separate events happening simultaneously. If that was true, then I do not have that ability. It happened quickly for me. One moment this crazy woman was screaming about how innocent Gwen was and the next, Gabby is falling to the ground bleeding and Oliver is wrestling a knife away from the psycho.

"Gabs? Gabby?" I knelt down beside my friend and looked for the wound, heedless of my skirt. It was in her side and bleeding badly.

"Fuck me that hurts." She tried to laugh but groaned instead. "Oh. Nursing school does not prepare you for being on the opposite end of shit."

"I can't imagine it does." I took off the blazer I was wearing and held it to her stomach. "I don't know what to do."

"It's okay." She tried to get control of her breathing. "Just keep pressure on it."

"Okay." I looked up. Twyla was still struggling. Silas had finally joined Oliver in trying to subdue her. No one else was helping, the crowd just stood there gaping. "Zu. Call an ambulance."

"Done." Zu turned her back on the noise and pulled out her cellphone.

"Weird." Gabby pulled my hand to her. "You need to press down a little more."

"Yeah, of course." I repositioned my hands. She placed one of hers over them. "What's weird?"

"This. I've never even broken a bone." She groaned. "Nope. I go straight to being stabbed." I grabbed one of her hands and held it gently, still trying to stop the bleeding.

"We have the same scar." I held up her palm and showed her. "I never noticed that before." She also had a thin white line going across her palm, but it was on her left hand, not her right like mine. "That's weird. How did you get yours? Never mind. Don't talk. We'll talk later."

I tried to keep pressure on the wound. The material of my blazer was not that absorbent. Blood was everywhere. "Fucking rayon."

"Rayon? You sold a painting for a million and you're wearing a rayon skirt and blazer?" Gabby laughed. "Cotton or wool next time. Just in case. Better at absorbing blood."

"Hopefully, there won't be a next time," I told her. "Now hold still. The ambulance will be here soon, okay?" For some reason, I could not look at her face. I was terrified that she would die, and I didn't want to see the light go out of those expressive brown eyes.

"Great. I've never ridden in the back of one. This should be fun." Her voice was strong. She was coherent. She was also amazingly calm. I was close to all out panicking.

"Oh, my god! What happened here?" Mrs. Hawkins asked as she made her way to us. "What the hell?"

"Twyla stabbed Gabby," I explained. "Zu's called an ambulance."

"He never wanted this. He never wanted any of this." She began crying. I could not pay attention to her. I was doing my best to keep pressure on Gabby's wound. I could not let my one and only true friend die. Again. "You were all like our children. It's what made what had to happen so sad. The whole thing just went *zbres bejecks suenatl…*"

"Mrs. Hawkins?" Someone grabbed her. I looked up in time to see her eyes roll and watched as she lost consciousness.

"Zu! Where's the ambulance?" Gabby was getting really pale. It scared me. "Gabby. Gabriella. Stay with me."

"I'm here, boss. I'm here." She patted my arm, but I barely felt it. Everything seemed as if I were in the middle of a fog with only streaks of light and color coming through. "I'm trying."

"Coming through. What happened?" A large, burly man removed my hands from Gabby's wound and tossed the ruined blazer aside.

"She was stabbed. I don't know how deep, but she's lost a lot of blood," I told him.

"What's your name, sweetheart?" He opened her eyes and shone a light into them. "Can you tell me your name?"

"It's Gabby. Her name is Gabby," I answered, not giving Gabby an opportunity to do so, as if speaking would be the death blow. She struggled to sit up, but the emergency tech easily pushed her back down.

"Okay. Thanks. Fred. We need to get her inside, stat," he hollered at the second EMT. The other one was hovering above Mrs. Hawkins.

"I think this one's had a stroke, Tony," the other man called. What was left of the crowd began speaking all at once, some into cell phones, others to one another.

My own limbs felt heavy. The bright day seemed to dim. The only color I could see was the red of Gabby's blood on my hands. I felt sick to my stomach. My head was bursting, I had a horrible taste of familiarity at the back of my throat.

"This one's been stabbed. Can't tell how badly," he told the other man tersely.

"She's a nurse. She works in Memphis in the ER." I hoped this bit of information would sway them, make them hurry. I had always heard of professional courtesy. I wanted to see it in action.

"Damn. We can't take them both. Get Roger to get his ass here quick," the EMT, Tony, who was working on Gabby instructed. "Is the other one stable?"

"Seems to be. She's not conscious and her breathing is shallow, but she's got a fairly steady pulse." He took a moment to holler into his radio and then listen as the static crackled. As usual, it hurt my head. "Roger's here. Let's get the young lady to the hospital."

I stood and watched as they loaded Gabby onto a stretcher. They put her on oxygen and placed a compression bandage on her wound. A small part of me winced as they ripped her shirt to get a better look at it. I knew the loss of a shirt was the least of her worries, but I knew she would be upset by it anyway.

"Claire?" Silas grabbed my attention. I didn't see him standing in front of me. "Come on. We're going to follow the ambulance."

"Yeah. Of course." I looked down at the blood on my hands and started shaking. There was so much of it. There should not have been so much of it. It was everywhere. The sand was red. I blinked. There was no sand here.

"Snap out of it, Claire. Come on. You can do it." He took me by the shoulders and got me to focus on him. "I know. I know that void is there, and you want to take a running leap into it. I see it every day. Stay with me, Gabby needs you. We need you."

"I'm okay." It took a long moment to pull my attention back from wherever it had gone. "I'm okay. I just need something to drink when we get there, okay?"

"I'll buy you a soda. I promise." He put his arm around me and helped me to the car. "Zu is going to bring Oliver. I picked him up so he wouldn't get his suit dirty on the motorcycle."

"You're a good friend, Silas. We are friends, right?" Half of my mind was floating. There was water and it was warm. The seagulls and waves were audible to me. The air smelled salty. I really wanted to be there. The other half of me was anchored in Silas's car and worried about my friend.

"Of course, we're friends, Claire. We've been friends since fifth grade, don't you remember?"

"Yeah. I just tend to forget, I guess." I leaned my head back on the seat and tried to keep my focus on the present. It was difficult. My vision wanted to go black. Everything shifted in and out of focus and my pulse could not decide which beat it wanted to follow, so it followed them all at once.

"I know. That's why I'm always there to remind you of who you are and what you did. You'll forget otherwise."

"What? What?" His voice sounded like it was underwater but also right in the middle of my ear.

"You okay to make it inside?" We were there before I realized we had left the cemetery and arrived at the hospital. Normally, that would bother me.

"Yeah. I think so." Words were thick and unwieldy. I felt as if there was something else we had been talking about. Something else we should have been talking about.

The automatic doors opened for us. Silas steered me to a seat in the waiting area and approached the front desk. While he was there, Zu and Oliver arrived. Zu sat next to me and held my hand. She knew how close Gabby and I were. She was a bit reserved like my mother, but I knew she was worried, as well.

"They're not letting anyone back there with her. She is likely to go straight to surgery," Silas said when he returned. "I've told them to let us know immediately how it goes. They're calling her parents, too."

"Good. I don't want to make that call." I think I said it aloud. I had always gotten along well with Gabby's mother and stepfather, but that was too personal a call to make. I couldn't face another friend's mother after causing her harm.

Minutes passed or maybe hours. I was not sure. Silas made good on his promise and bought me a soda. It helped. The carbonation and caffeine kicked my senses in the rear, and it became easier to live in the world around me. It helped that the ubiquitous TV in the lobby was broken. The only sounds were the normal ones like beeps, coughs, whispers, ticks from the giant clock on the wall and the hiss of the automatic doors. It was soothing, much more so than silence would have been.

More people in funeral attire arrived. Mrs. Hawkins was brought in just after Gabby. However, the older woman was not going in for surgery. They rushed her to get a CT-scan. If the overheard whispers were true, she had suffered a stroke right after the service. That explained why her phrasing and voice went odd.

"Any idea what happened to Twyla?" Zu asked sometime later.

"I heard they took her in for psych evaluation," Oliver told us. "Someone outside the bathroom was talking about it on the phone. Apparently, she had been committed before. I didn't ask."

"Yeah, it's not like they'll talk to us." Silas stated as he rejoined us. He kept getting up and pacing every few minutes.

"I heard someone blame us for it. I guess we're into hoodoo or voodoo or whatever now," Zu said scornfully.

"Mrs. Hawkins said that he never wanted this." I felt my strength returning. My curiosity was awake, and I wanted answers. "Said that we were like their children. She knows something important. I think she was about to say something important when she collapsed. He was in on it somehow and she knew."

"How? He wasn't there, Claire." Oliver scratched the stubble on his cheek.

"Could have been. I have no idea. It's a big island," Silas admitted. "Look, Claire obviously believes he had something to do with it. Let's explore that."

"I agree. They didn't have kids," I told him. "Why does my gut say he was involved?"

"You reckon anyone will be home?" he asked. The other two just stared at us.

"Let's find out." I smiled. I felt daring and excited.

"What are you planning?" Zu asked.

"We are not planning anything, Ms. Attorney," I told her. "But Silas and I are going to go searching for a few clues, later, since no one is home."

"You can't break in." Oliver's voice caught and rose an octave. "That's nuts."

"We can and we will," Silas said. "While we do that, you two see if you can find anything at your houses. Maybe someone kept the newspaper articles and stuff."

"The library should have all that too," Zu said. "But this is nuts, like Oliver said. Silas, why are you—?

"Silas, buddy, really—" Oliver started at the same time.

"Claire, weren't you talking to Gwen's sister?" Silas asked me.

"Yeah." I thought I knew where he was going with this. "I could maybe see if she knows anything, but she was nine."

"But I hear the chase and uncertainty drove her mother crazy. She may still have any information that her mother had collected," he argued.

"Okay. Fine. We all have jobs to do. Let's wait and make sure Gabby's going to make it before we jump up and go all Nancy Drew on it." I was not ready to leave without knowing that she would survive this ugly day.

"Her parents are there. I just saw a doctor talk to them." Zu nudged me. "Let's go see what he told them."

"Ms. Anna?" I said quietly when we got close enough. Heads turned to watch us. I could feel the weight of their stares. "Ms. Anna? How is she?"

"She's going to make it. They said it didn't hit anything important. She'll be okay." Ms. Anna looked at me with tears in her eyes. "The doctor, he said that they're going to stitch it up if they can't glue it and let her go."

"They said she'll sleep for a while when she gets home. When they move back from ultrasound, before the stitch, they're gonna let us see her," her stepdad said. "It was nice of you waiting."

"Gabby is the best friend I have. Of course, I'm going to be here," I told him. "I am going to head home to clean up and get something to eat now, though. Can I get you anything? Bring you something back?" They looked so small and frightened. It hit me pretty hard.

"No, thank you. That's so sweet, Claire." Her mother patted my arm. "You take care of yourself now. We'll let you know if anything changes, okay? And you'll be back to see her?"

"Certainly. Thank you." I stepped back to the others. Since they didn't know Gabby's parents, they left me to be the group spokesperson. "Okay. Let's get out of here." I just wanted to go home, get blisteringly drunk, and sleep for days. But there were a few things I had to do first.

Chapter Ten

I cut the lights as I pulled into the parking space and looked at the building in front of me. I fought the urge to be sick as much as fought the urge to run away. I had not made a plan. Unless it was to paint, I never made plans. No one else knew I was here, alone.

"Shit," I muttered. I unplugged my cellphone, opened the voice recorder app I had downloaded, one that encrypted everything it saved, and walked inside. I had to know. I could not sleep, and I had to know.

The automated doors didn't open automatically. I put my hands in my jacket pockets, pulled my hood up and walked around to the side. Nurses usually take breaks. People who were visiting or staying with a patient late would eventually leave. I searched for a likely after hours exit and found one around the backside of the building. It was dark there with just one streetlight and a lone bare bulb on the building. There were also a lot of hedges running the length of the building. I could see the purpose of them. They ran under the windows of every room. It was a deterrent to sneak out of the place. It was not necessarily a way to stop someone from sneaking inside.

The first time the door opened, it was a loud group of people. I nodded to them, acting as if I were merely taking a break outside. It was a long hour of waiting and taking hits from my flask before my patience was rewarded when a young woman in scrubs came outside. She had a phone to her ear and a pack of cigarettes in her hand. She didn't see me. I grabbed the door and slipped in before it closed.

I had never been inside the hospital's off-site psych center before. It looked very much like an office building gave birth to a dormitory. There were rooms and offices along each wall. Some had placards on the door sharing the name of the residents inside. Most of them had signs directing visitors to knock before opening a door. They had painted it a dull, light gray, which did a poor job of disguising the cinder blocks. Even the air seemed heavy. I had to fight back memories from a different time and place.

Twyla's room was near the front, if the people I had overheard in the hospital were to be believed. There was a nursing station between me and her room. It had a convenient sign on the wall directing people to its existence. I inched around to see if anyone was standing there. I didn't see anything. The end of the hallway had one of those large mirrors parking garages use to let people know when another car is coming. I checked it and saw myself. The desk looked empty, which was good since I was pretty sure anyone at the desk would have seen me in the mirror had they looked at it.

Nevertheless, I walked as softly as possible, rolling my feet marching band style to keep from making any noise. I had no idea if I would be allowed to see Twyla, but I doubted it. Most places like this had strict policies about visitors. I doubted I would have been on the list of her visitors, so I was sneaky and safe rather than bold and possibly being escorted out of the place by security.

I found Twyla's room and listened as long as I dared for the telltale signs of other people in there before easing it open and closing it gently behind me. Twyla was not the only occupant. The other person in the room was lying on one side and facing the door. I could not tell anything about the other person, gender identity, ethnicity, mental ability or biological status. I had no idea who or what, living or dead, was in the room with us. I had known that was possible, but it didn't keep my heart rate from skyrocketing.

"You're not really Gwen's friend, you know," Twyla said conversationally.

I swear I jumped a foot. It took me a minute to find her even though she was sitting up looking at the door.

"How so?" I asked. I was paying more attention to calming down than I was to what she had said. I pulled out my flask and took a larger than normal gulp. There were times I liked the burn.

"If you had been a true friend, you wouldn't have come back without her. You'd have stayed, too." I had been around people with varying degrees of mental illness before, so I was accustomed to hearing strange claims, but this one threw me a little.

"What do you mean by that?" I asked.

"Whenever I see her, she's so mad that you didn't stay with her." Twyla's voice changed and regressed. She sounded almost childlike. It was scary on a whole other level. "Why didn't you stay with her, Claire? I would have, but they didn't want me."

"Who?" I started doubting my intentions. The rumors had always said that Twyla was off, that she had severe mental health issues. I didn't know why I could not chalk her act of violence on my friend to that. It had been perfectly logical, and everyone else had swallowed it. Maybe that had been my problem. I could not always accept logical outcomes. I was poor at math. I had failed higher-level sciences and I had never been good with those mental challenges teachers liked to give out in school. I sucked at thinking critically unless I was criticizing something. Of course, I knew that wasn't the same thing.

"You know who, stupid." She sat up in bed and waved me closer. "Them. They have her and they want us all to fight in their war. It's going to be massive."

"Really?" I was trapped.

"Yeah." She waved me closer, her voice barely more than a whisper. I went cautiously. "They need soldiers, but they said I can't be one because I talked about them. So, they put me in here. You shouldn't have left Gwen, though. She's sad. She misses you guys. She knows you loved her. She told me that. She thought when they took you up back then that you would finally stay. But you never stay. You love her, but you always leave."

"I wasn't in love with Gwen," I said loudly. I had forgotten where I was standing for a moment. The old denial roared to be free. "I wasn't even attracted to Gwen."

"Liar." Twyla grabbed me close and roughly pressed her mouth to mine. I lost my balance as she pulled me forward.

It took all I had to break free from her grasp as my hands found the wall and the bed. I pushed away violently. I was not quick enough to escape the slap. Twyla had long fingernails. They left marks on my cheek. I could feel the sting and pain.

"What the hell did you do that for?" I asked. It was stupid. I should have turned around then and left as quickly and quietly as I could. However, I didn't.

"I'll save you for her. We'll all be together," Twyla exclaimed loudly. She tried to get out of her bed.

"The hell is going on?" A smoke roughened voice came from the other bed. An older woman with thinning white hair sat up and screamed when she saw me. Twyla pulled the alarm.

"Goddamn it." I really was trapped. Not knowing what else to do, I hurried to the window. It was sealed shut.

I panicked. The window had been my escape route. I had no choice but to fling the door open and make a run for it. I had parked a short distance from the entrance. I made it to my car and got it cranked before young men in scrubs and an older man in a security officer's uniform were exiting the front doors. I threw the car in reverse and floored it. I didn't slow down until I was back on the highway heading home.

Bayview was near a military base. Residents were accustomed to seeing low flying planes and helicopters all the time. However, as I pulled onto the highway, I noticed one flying parallel to my car. It was a helicopter, or at least that is what I thought it was, and it had very bright lights on it. It was eerily quiet. It stayed close to me until we got closer to town. Then it went higher and I lost it in the clouds. I was certain it was still there, however.

It was late. I had grabbed my laptop bag before I left the house. It had a sketchbook and headphones in it. I didn't want to go home. The helicopter unnerved me. Instead of heading to the house, I went straight to Mabel's for coffee. It was open, well-lit and there were always people around. Short of one of the twenty-four-hour retail chains, it was the safest place of which I could think.

My cheek stung where Twyla had hit me. I checked in the mirror. The scratches were visible. It looked as if a few had bled. I found a napkin and cleaned what I could. I used a liberal amount of whisky on a napkin as antiseptic. It would have been just my luck to die because of an infection from some mental patient's fingernails. It stung like hell. Finally free of blood and confident in alcohol's healing abilities, I went inside.

"Back again?" the woman behind the counter asked as I walked inside.

"Pardon me?" I felt a strange sense of déjà vu, it was true, but I highly doubted I had been in there at night this trip.

"You were here this morning with Stephanie," the woman explained. "I had come in to get the previous night's receipts."

"Okay." I had no idea who that person was or why she was speaking to me.

"It's okay. You look like I'm about to attack you." She laughed and pulled out a coffee mug, filled it and sat it on the counter. "I'm Erin. I own the place. I know Stephanie through mutual friends."

"Ah." It didn't set my mind at ease.

"You're Claire, right?" She laughed again when I nodded. "Come sit down. It's okay. I'm not going to poison you. For one thing, I don't believe the rumors that go around this town. For another, I was here when whatever happened, happened. I didn't believe it then, I don't believe it now. You're good. Sit. Have a cup on the house."

"Thanks." I took tentative steps to the counter and sat down. "Not many people who are from here are so accepting." I added creamer to the coffee and watched it swirl. I always liked watching it mix together. It was a little like paint that way.

"A lot of people around here have their heads up their collective asses." She offered me a menu. "Hungry? The cook is on break, but I can still make a mean omelet."

"No thanks. You don't look like a Mabel, but you do look familiar." I placed my laptop bag on the chair beside me and got comfortable. It did bother me to have my back to the door, but I felt safe there. Aside from Erin, there were several other people in the place. Instinctively I knew that if anyone was following me, helicopter or not, they would not attempt anything in public place with witnesses.

"Mabel died years ago. And truthfully, she wasn't running this place for years before that," she explained. "Are you okay? Looks like a cat or something larger got you."

"Yeah. Cat," I lied. I hated to blame Vinnie, but I didn't want to explain to a stranger why I had scratches on my cheek.

"Dog person myself. Don't get cats," she said.

"Oh." There didn't seem to be anything to add there. "Thanks for the coffee."

"Don't mention it. I see you brought stuff with you. I'll let you do what it is you do." She pulled a cloth out from somewhere beneath the counter and walked to one of the booths.

It was pretty late. I had no one to call with Gabby in the hospital and Lane asleep. He didn't keep the same hours I did, plus he had gone to the East Coast to visit family, so it was even later there. Instead, I called Silas.

As we made plans to meet the next day, I pulled out my sketchbook and let my hand have free reign. Sometimes free drawing helped ease my general anxiety, or at least allowed enough energy to escape that I would be able to sleep with or without alcohol. When our plans to meet were made, I let him go. I was not in the mood for idle chatter suddenly.

"Need a refill?" Erin asked a few moments later. "Wow. That's really good."

"Huh?" I looked down first at my cup and then at my sketchbook. I had sketched the counter complete with my coffee cup. "Oh. Thanks. So, how much?" I asked as I reached into my bag for my wallet.

"It's on the house." She waved me off.

"Thanks." I told her again. I caught her looking down at the sketch again. I signed my name to it and tore it out of the book. "Fair trade."

"I can't accept that," she protested.

"It's for the coffee. It probably cost me the same thing as giving me a free cup of coffee did you," I argued. "Take it."

"Thanks. I'll have to get it framed." She held it up to the light. "Thanks, Claire."

"Have a good night." I pulled my bag on my shoulder and left. I had another sly outing planned for the next night. I knew I needed sleep, so I made my way home and to bed, staying up only long enough to get really drunk so I could fall asleep.

Chapter Eleven

I woke up the next afternoon with a pounding headache and an unaccustomed soreness in my face. I staggered to the bathroom to see three angry red lines on my cheek. Twyla had marked me. I hadn't dreamed it.

My hair fell loose around my shoulders. I didn't feel much like taking a shower, so I pulled it back into some semblance of a ponytail. It was out of my face, anyway.

It was later than I normally slept, by hours, but I figured the events of the prior evening had taken a toll. The whole thing, being at the funeral, the stabbing, the hospital, it had all be so dramatic and exhausting.. I checked my phone and found a few texts from Gabby and one from Silas. I called him first.

"You still want to sneak into the Hawkins house?" He didn't even say hi first. He just jumped right to the point.

"Yeah. I have to know. You sure you're okay with doing this?"

"It wouldn't be the first time you and I broke into a place. Remember?"

"Vaguely." I hadn't until he mentioned it. I could almost see us breaking into his cousin's house for some odd reason. I don't remember what we did it for though. I got the feeling it wasn't the only place we had entered illegally.

"Well, I still remember how to do it. Wanna meet for an early dinner? We shouldn't get out there until after dark."

"Yeah, that'd be fine. You can drive since you know the way."

"Want me to pick you up?"

"No. I'll walk down to Crosby's. Do you know where that is?" I don't know why I picked Stephanie's restaurant, but it felt right.

"Yeah. It's a block and a half from Mabel's, isn't it?"

"It is."

"Cool. It fits. I'll meet you there in three hours. Sound good?"

"That's fine. I'll meet you there."

Three hours was the time I had to hang about. I didn't know what to do with that time. I debated going to the house for coffee but remembered my dad's orders to stay out from under his roof. Groaning, I fell back on the bed and grabbed my phone. I didn't feel like checking social media or my email. Instead, I set an alarm and closed my eyes. The alarm went off before I was aware I had fallen asleep.

The walk to Crosby's was a good way to wake up. The restaurant was nice. The tables matched the chairs. Local art was hanging on the walls and there was not a TV in sight. It also smelled amazing. As soon as I walked inside, I was hungry. Dinner apparently was a casual event. The sign at the hostess stand recommended that I seat myself. I didn't see Silas, so I chose a booth set slightly off from the rest of the tables.

"Can I help you?" the server asked as soon as I sat down.

"I'd like a glass of sweet tea, please." I was polite. I smiled and reached for the menu. That is when the shit started.

"You have some fucking nerve being here." I heard the voice, but I didn't realize it was directed at me. "Don't ignore me, you bitch. What the hell are you doing in here?"

"Pardon me?" I realized she was addressing me when a bread roll hit the menu I was examining.

"Oh. That got your attention. Don't you know who owns this place?" The woman was older than me with fake blonde hair and half inch long dark roots. The industrial strength false eyelashes she was wearing looked lethal.

"Stephanie Crosby," I answered calmly. I was hoping to avoid escalating the issue.

"Damn right. So, what the fuck are you doing here? You come to rub it in her face?"

"She invited me." I felt my heart pound and my vision narrowed.

"Bull shit." The woman stood and approached my table. "You really have fucking balls showing up here. I think you should leave."

"I don't think that's up to you." I didn't look at her. I didn't want a fight. I didn't want a scene, but that was beyond my control. "I just want to eat," I said weakly.

Spots were appearing before my eyes. It was too much. The confrontation after the escapades of the night before, coupled with the plans I was about to make for that night—too much. I felt anxiety well in me. I wanted to run, to hit, to scream or to curl into a tight ball under the covers and wait for it all to go away. My breathing hitched.

"I can't believe they let you out. You fucking bitch!" She pulled back and I waited on the punch or glass of liquid or whatever she had planned on throwing at me. Nothing came.

"I think *you* should leave." The soft voice came from behind me, but a rather tall man was holding the woman's hand back. It looked as if he had caught her in mid strike. "Thanks, Darin. I've got it from here."

"No problem, Stephanie." He smiled, released the woman's arm, and walked back to the kitchen.

"Like I said, I think you should leave," the chef stated firmly.

"I tried to get her to leave, Steph, but she is pretty damned stubborn." The woman seemed confident that I was about to be evicted from my seat.

"Claire can stay." Stephanie moved closer and put a warm hand on my shoulder and squeezed gently. "You need to leave, Denise."

"What the hell? You're throwing *me* out? Do you know who that is? What she did?" The woman sounded indignant.

"Denise, get out. Don't make me call Darin back up here. He's wanted to kick your ass out of here for years."

"Well, fuck this. And fuck you then." The woman, Denise, walked back to her table, grabbed her purse and left.

"Well, that could have gone worse," Stephanie said as she dropped into the booth across from me. Her white tunic had the restaurant's name embroidered on it.

"And my parents wonder why I don't come home more." I shook my head a little to clear the tension in my neck. "Thank you. You certainly didn't have to let me stay."

"Of course, I did! Denise will get past it or not. She only comes in because she's my cousin and the servers give her free food."

"You don't?" My heart rate was slowing but my hands were still shaking. I hid them in my lap. It confused me. She wasn't asking me to leave.

"Not if I can help it. She's always been a loudmouth, bigoted bitch," she said easily. I didn't hear any bitterness in the tone.

"Every family has one." It was the only thing I could think of to say. Though my mother had been an only child, my father had not. Some of his family had been a little less than accepting even before the accident. He, of course, had been much less accepting.

"Well, I am glad you decided to try my little establishment for dinner." She smiled. "Anything in particular you've been thinking about on the menu?"

"I haven't really gotten a chance to study it," I admitted.

"It's not a test, Claire." She laughed. It was a wonderful laugh and it made me smile in response. "Were you meeting someone here?"

"Silas. He's joining me for dinner." I regretted that. I knew she would get up and leave and I found myself not wanting her to do so.

"Cool. Better him than Oliver." Her smile faded. She didn't elaborate, and I didn't ask. I could only imagine what her parents must have said about each of us after it happened, and Oliver in particular.

"How much do you…?" I almost asked it. I almost asked how much she remembered, but Silas arrived and interrupted my train of thought.

"Dude, there's this woman with massive fake eyelashes and a real bad dye job throwing a huge tantrum outside. What happened?" he asked as he approached the table. "Oh. Stephanie, right? Silas Brown at your service."

"I remember you." Stephanie stood and shook his hand. "I'll get back to my cooking and let you two talk. Take a look at the menu. Don't be afraid to ask for something special either. If we have it, I can make it."

"Sweet. Thanks." He slid into the booth she had just left. "Great kid."

"I don't think she's a kid anymore," I told him. I tried and failed to keep from watching her walk back to the kitchen. Gwen certainly didn't have an ass like that.

"I see what you're thinking." He brought my attention back to the table. "You think that's wise?"

"I'm not doing anything," I told him. "I'm not planning anything. I'm not going to say anything. I was just appreciating the view." It took a little time to reacquaint myself to the air of comfort I had around Silas. It took a little longer to remember that I could tell him anything, even though he always reminded me of a frat house president, with unruly hair, a baby face, stocky build and slight chub, he was always open and fair-minded. It amazed me when I realized just how much I had missed him. I hadn't appreciated it until I'd seen him again.

"I'll allow that." He laughed. "So, what's the plan?"

"First, I want food. It smells amazing in here." I took another deep breath and tried to identify the smells. There was wood smoke, so obviously they had grill of some sort. There was the hint of garlic. I was a firm believer that a hint was not enough when it came to garlic. Most of all, there was the rich smell of gravy and well-crafted meats. It made my mouth water in a way food hadn't in a very long time.

"Oh man, it does. What do they do, place grilled garlic in every corner? They need to market that and sell it. Every house needs to smell like this." Silas appreciated good food.

"You're telling me." I looked quickly at the menu and decided on one of the specials, hamburger steak and gravy on rice with a salad, fries—because obviously fries—and corn on the cob. I had the feeling I was about to enjoy eating again. "I'm ready."

"Me, too." He put his menu down and looked around. The server was there in an instant. "So, I'd like to try the seafood special."

"Would you like your shrimp fried or grilled?" she asked.

"Grilled." He nodded as if it was a very tough question. It may have been for him. I hate seafood so I would not know.

"I'd like coke if you don't mind, regular, not diet," I requested after telling her my order. Apparently, the earlier ruckus had canceled my previously ordered sweet tea. "Thank you."

"You are welcome. Your salads will be right up." She placed her pad in her apron and walked into the kitchen.

"So, what is the special of the day?" I asked. I had not even looked at the seafood part of the menu.

"Flounder stuffed with crabmeat topped with shrimp and a homemade remoulade sauce." He looked at me. "I forgot, you hate seafood."

"I do. That made prom a little weird, didn't it?" I laughed.

Silas and I had doubled with Oliver and Gwen. He had been a good sport about it even knowing that it wasn't an official date. By that point, I had realized I liked girls more than boys. Ironically, I had been dating him at that time and he was the first person I had talked to about it.

"It did. Well, that's what we got for making reservations at a seafood restaurant before double checking with our dates." He shrugged. "I promise I have not made the same mistake since."

"Do you date much?" I asked. I was eager to know if everyone in our groups had horrible luck in their love life. I was heartily sick of mine, and I desperately wanted something, anything on which to blame it. I believed it would have helped if I had known I was not alone.

"Sometimes. Certainly not for long." Silas leaned back against the booth as if stretching. "You want to know something weird?"

"Everything is weird," I said, half in jest. "What?"

"I can't seem to talk to people like normal. It's always like there's a wall between everyone and me. It doesn't seem like that with you guys though."

"Wonder if that's because we share the tragedy of no remembrance." I rolled my eyes. "Honestly, though, Gabby is the only person I'm close to. All my relationships end in failure. I have a cat and I have a few people I can deal with in short bursts, like my friend Lane. He's a writer and I do a lot of illustrating stuff for him."

"Children's books?" I couldn't tell if he had a tone or if he was just being Silas.

"Graphic novels." It's not awkward to admit that to him. I knew he would not have thought less of me for it.

"I tried to work outside my dad's company, but my anxiety was so bad I couldn't. All I really do is sit in a few meetings, take some conference calls and add a few numbers around here and there." He shrugged. "Nepotism has its privileges."

"At least it lets you live away from here." I nodded at the table Denise had been sitting at earlier, even though he had not witnessed it.

"True, but as much shit as we get when we're here, my mind feels clearer than anywhere else. And I've been to the Himalayas."

"I do feel less anxious around you guys. I haven't had much to drink at all today." I almost didn't realize that. "But it's early yet." I didn't tell him I was still a little hungover from the night before. By the time I had passed out, I had finished almost a fifth of vodka and a full bottle of orange juice.

"Naysayer to the end." He laughed. "If I were a lesbian, we'd be married."

"That's one I haven't heard before." I laughed, as well.

"At least I didn't take it personally, you coming out and all." He stopped laughing. "I guess I kinda knew it when we were going together. You were just all into hanging out with Gabby and Gwen. Oliver always thought you were in love with Gwen. He wasn't mad about it though. We all kinda knew. I can't believe you let me talk you into having sex." He laughed softly.

"Did we have sex? I honestly don't remember." I didn't pay attention to the other thing he said. I was used to hearing it, inaccurate as it was. It surprised me that it didn't seem to hurt his feelings, at least he gave no sign that it did. "If we did, it was to test whether or not I liked penis, I guess."

"I can see that. I don't get it. I didn't have to fuck a guy to realize I'm not gay," he pointed out.

"Yeah, but the times and the pressure and parents." I sighed and rubbed my head. "You know, I have trouble remembering a lot of high school."

"Me, too. It's something else that seems clearer when I'm here." He leaned back in the booth and put his arm across the top. "I get really weird headaches and odd feelings when I try to remember what happened to us. In fact, it's so bad I've just kinda given up and let the idea go that I'll ever know what you did."

"Here are your salads. Stephanie's working on your entrees as we speak. They'll be right out." The server placed our salads in front of us along with two large glasses of carbonated beverage.

"Thank you." I looked at Silas again. He had moved his plate toward him and salted it. "Did you say what I did?"

"No. What are you talking about?"

"You said what I did."

"I said what we did. Really, Claire. Have you been taking your meds?"

"Yes." I shook my head to clear it. I looked around and made sure the server was out of earshot. I didn't want anyone to hear us as we planned things. "You know where they live, right?"

"Yeah. It's an old house out in the middle of nowhere," he told me as he meticulously began cutting up his salad. "We can park down the road and walk up so we don't attract anyone's attention. There's a lot that's been partially cleared where we can leave the car."

"Excellent. What time is good for you?" It was a plan. I knew, we both did, that it could have turned out with nothing, but we needed action. We needed to do something, besides my excursion to see Twyla.

"I thought we were going after this. It'll be dark but not too late that we'll raise eyebrows when we get back. You good with that?"

"Yes. It sounds good to me." I carefully mixed my salad. I liked to bathe the lettuce in the dressing. "What all do you remember about high school? Do you have gaps, too, or is it just about that weekend?"

"I have a lot of lost weekends, that's just one of many. I do remember several times we ended up in places we shouldn't have been."

"Oh, yeah? Want to remind me?"

"Entrees?" The server reappeared and placed our entrees down as a busser took the salad plates. I wasn't done with mine, but that was okay. I found myself eager to try my food. I took up a forkful, waiting politely until we were alone again.

"Of course. Holy shit, this is good." Silas didn't wait. He took a bite of his fish before the server asked if we needed anything else. She left quickly. "Long as she can stand us, I think I'll be eating here a lot."

"Me, too." It really was good. The hamburger steak was tender, and the gravy had been so flavorful that it just seemed to melt together into a blob of awesomeness.

"So, what was the dust up about when I walked in? Why was that lady outside so pissed?" he asked instead of treating me to a trip down memory lane.

"Oh, that." I told him what he had missed. He seemed disappointed he had not been there for it. "So, she got kicked out instead. I got to stay and have this amazing meal."

"Good. Man, sometimes I hate people." He looked at his cellphone as it rang. "Work calls. You mind if I take this? I get in trouble if I miss too many conference calls."

"No. Go ahead." I didn't mind. It gave me the chance to finish my meal without it getting cold. It really was good. I found myself wanting to savor it and then immediately order another serving for later.

While Silas listened to his phone and made non-committal answers and grunts, I finished my meal and pulled out my own phone. I checked my email to find that Lane had approved all the pages I had sent. All that was left was shading. It was a black and white graphic novel and without color, it would predispose one into believing it would be an easier job drawing it. It was not. Shading took on epic meaning, and it was something I didn't let anyone else do. Perhaps that was why I worked freelance and mainly with Lane. There was not as much pressure on a deadline with him as there would have been at an established company.

Silas's phone call didn't take too long. I was amused that he continued eating while listening to it. The power of the mute button was undeniable. We didn't linger after we finished. Stephanie didn't come out and see us off. It was getting crowded, so I guessed the dinner rush was upon her.

Chapter Twelve

It was cloudy and dark. It was slightly cool, as well. I was thankful for my hoodie. I had taken the precaution of wearing dark clothes. When Silas showed up in similar attire, I was relieved.

I let him drive. He knew where we were going better than I did and his car was a darker color. Silas was a good driver, careful and not prone to speeding. We rode in silence, which was a relief. I do not know if he was nervous, but I was. It had been a long time since I had broken into a house. A fact I hadn't remembered until he reminded me.

We parked about a block away from the house. We drove by it first and made sure no one was home. All the lights were out but there was a car in the driveway. It looked promising.

"Okay. Ready?" Silas asked as we carefully closed the car doors.

"As I'll ever be." I shouldered the small backpack I used as a purse in case we found something that needed to be brought out of the house.

"Here." He handed me a small flashlight. "Might need this."

"I don't know. Is that a good idea? Skulking around with a flashlight?"

"Who knows? It's been a long time since I've done this."

"Me, too." He had reminded me at dinner that when we had dated briefly in high school, I had joined him in some of the elaborate pranks he would play on members of his family and certain friends. A lot of these pranks involved sneaking into locked houses, boats, sheds and other places we were not supposed to be late at night. I remember mostly being the getaway driver. However, there were vague images of being more involved in some of the tricks. We had gotten pretty good at it, and the tricks seemed harmless enough.

We walked through the wooded section that divided the properties. Mr. Hawkins kept his lot wooded. It seemed safer than walking down the road. At least there were fewer open areas. There were a lot of low hanging branches and roots that were unexpectedly underfoot.

We made it around behind the house without incident. The French doors leading to the back patio were sturdy and heavily bolted. However, the windows were older. It took just a pop of Silas's pocketknife to get the window off track and able to open. We were fortunate. The rod they had placed there to stop this from happening was too short. Silas held my backpack as I climbed through.

I used the flashlight to navigate the hallway. The French doors were bolted with a key lock, but the key was hanging on a hook just inside the door. It was almost too easy. It set me on edge.

Sylvia Hawkins had decorated her house very provincially. I scanned the walls carefully with the flashlight and noticed the outdated wallpaper. There were bunnies. It had worse. There were groups of pale green bunnies sitting or cavorting in bunches of tall grass. It was horrid.

"What exactly are we looking for?" Now that we were there, I was second-guessing the wisdom of our plan.

"Sylvia said that he was distraught about what happened to us, to Gwen. Personally, I've always kinda blamed him but I don't know why," Silas whispered.

"Me either. A lot of my memories of him are blurred." That was true. I didn't know if it was from chronological distance or something else, but I had a hard time remembering a lot of stuff, especially if Mr. Hawkins had been involved in that memory.

"It's almost like someone or something modified our memories." He felt under his nose. "That's odd. Usually, I get a nosebleed just thinking about conspiracies."

"Let's check and see if he had an office or something." I didn't feel comfortable being in a dark house in the middle of nowhere talking about conspiracies.

The house was a typical ranch style. The kitchen where I had let Silas in, had a small breakfast area, which was open to a long, rectangular living room. Above it was the formal dining room. Four bedrooms and a bath were down the long, dark hallway. The hall was labeled in dark wood and covered with dusty pictures. The entire house seemed to be tiled. We walked softly.

The smallest bedroom, on the left, was set up as a home office. It was not the room I had entered, but it was across from it. This room faced the road. As it turned out, it was a good thing it did.

"Find anything?" I asked as Silas searched through a filing cabinet. I was checking the desk.

"I can't tell." It was muffled because he had his flashlight in his mouth. "Hang on. This may be something."

"Not a damn thing here." I sighed in frustration. I began opening drawers in the desk. The top drawer was locked. "You got a pocketknife?"

"Yeah. You don't? Isn't it a law that all lesbians carry one?" he asked as he handed me his. "Shit. Kill the light."

"What?" I turned off the flashlight but used the blade of the pocketknife to jimmy the lock.

"Someone just pulled in." He quickly crouched down and looked out the window. "Hopefully, they'll turn around. Shit, they're not turning around. We got to go."

"Hang on." I rammed my hand into the drawer and pulled out the first and only thing I touched. It was a book. I glanced briefly into the drawer. It was the only thing in there. It had to be important. "Let's go."

Several things happened at one time. All the lights came on in the house. The fire alarms began wailing and the TV's turned themselves on to very static laden channels. Silas's nose started bleeding, and I was almost knocked to my knees with a killer headache.

"We gotta get out of here." I read his lips. I had clapped my hands on my ears as soon as the noise started.

"Go." I nodded to him. He threw the folder he was holding into the backpack. I tossed the book and flashlight in there, as well.

Usually when I hear a lot of static, my mind tries to make out words in the noise. I didn't have time, but part of me wanted to stop moving. It sounded like my name, like the static was calling me. I could tell it affected Silas the same way. He would look at the TV in the bedroom we ran into as if mesmerized.

"Through the window," he whispered hoarsely. "You first."

"All right." I boosted myself up with my hands as he opened the window and then I was over and out. It was not too bad for someone my age.

I waited, pressed against the brick wall, trying to be small and invisible. It seemed like forever before one of Silas's legs came through shortly followed by the other. He was not as agile as he had been when we were kids. He closed the window back and stood panting beside me.

"Shit." Suddenly there were dogs barking and it was close. Light seemed to hover above us too, as if someone on the roof was looking for us with a spotlight. "How fast can you run?" I asked.

"Guess we're about to find out." He looked up, pulled on the backpack and motioned for me to go ahead. He didn't need to tell me twice.

We raced through the cleared area of the house's backyard until we got to the trees. It was tempting to slow down at that point, but a loud crack and a yell stopped that idea. I didn't look at him. I just ran as fast as I could through the trees, ducking under branches and trying not to get tripped up by roots. I had misjudged badly and worn flats. Not my brightest moment.

There was another crack and pine needles rained down on us. I didn't need further evidence to know that someone was shooting at us. We could hear the dogs chasing us even above the sound of our own panting. I was more scared at that moment than I ever had been before.

Finally, we reached the car. Silas had backed into the trees. He unlocked it with a key fob as we ran. I pulled open the door and threw myself inside. He slid across the hood, fell and then jumped in behind the steering wheel. In seconds we were safely inside a running vehicle. I looked back and saw more lights coming from above and a tall man walking toward us with a shotgun.

"Punch it!" I yelled. "Fuck the dogs, run them over if you have to, just go."

"That's what I'm doing!" He slammed his foot on the accelerator and didn't slow down until we were several streets away.

"Fuck me, someone was shooting at us!" I said when I finally caught my breath.

"Run over the dogs?" He looked at me.

"What the fuck ever, I'm a cat person." I could not help it. I laughed. So did he. It was a nice release from the stress.

"Think whoever that was knows it was us?" he asked finally.

"I hope not." I thought about it pretty hard. "I don't think so. That wasn't Sylvia, obviously. Think it was whoever may be involved in whatever the fuck this is?"

"I don't know. But honestly, right now, tell me something."

"What?"

"Did you hear your name in the static, too?" He looked straight ahead at the road when he asked that. I watched, but he didn't flick his eyes in my direction. It had scared him.

"Yes. I did. Sometimes, when my TV goes all crazy with the static or I couldn't get a radio signal, I think perhaps I can hear voices in it." I had not admitted that to anyone after my first therapist thought I should have been committed for it. He thought I was a paranoid schizophrenic. Sometimes I wished he had been correct. At least there was medication for that.

"Okay. So, it's not just me then. Good." He looked relieved. "I can work with that. That puts one of my pet theories out the window, though. I'm not sure how an international pedophile ring would control static."

"Dude, really? We were all of age or nearly." The thought sickened me. "That is just sick that you even went there."

"I didn't immediately. It was suggested," he said in defense. "And who's to say that shit doesn't happen?"

"Subject change. Are you going home after this?" I repressed a shudder.

"Back to my house, you mean or home like back to Chicago?"

"Back to your house here."

"Yeah. I'm going to stick this out. Like you, I can't live without knowing any longer. Besides, someone has to help you break into places."

"True." I had not noticed until I looked up that we were stopped in my driveway. "Ok then. I guess we'll convene and discuss the materials later?"

"Yeah, we should have Zu and Ollie with us. Gabby too, of course. Have you talked to her today?"

"No. I don't think so. I mean, I didn't talk to her." It took me a moment to understand what he was asking.

"Go home. Get some rest. We just had the shit scared out of us. We'll figure it out later."

"Good plan. Goodnight, Silas. Drive safe." I got the backpack from the floorboard and pulled it onto my shoulder.

"Goodnight, Claire."

Chapter Thirteen

I didn't sleep well that night. I kept feeling as if someone was watching me. As a precaution, before I went to sleep, I unplugged all the electronics. I was a bit spooked.

I hid the backpack in the trunk of my car, under the spare after using my pocket scanner on the notebook. I tried to make sure no one saw me when I put it in there. I hid the electronic copies in the cloud and another copy on a memory stick. After being chased by dogs and shot at, I didn't feel I was being too cautious.

After properly hiding the backpack, I went for my morning run. As usual, I ended up at Mabel's for breakfast. Stephanie was there, sitting in a booth. She waved and gestured for me to join her.

"Morning. You look tired." She, on the other hand, looked far too comfortable with being awake at such an hour.

"Thanks." I shrugged. "You certainly know how to sweet talk a girl."

"I didn't mean..." She blushed. It was adorable. I had to remind myself that I had been there when her sister disappeared all those years ago and last night I had been chased by dogs and shot at. It was not the time to fantasize. However, I really did want it to be. It was a nice distraction.

"I know. I didn't sleep well last night."

"When is the last time you had a good night's sleep?"

"I really don't know," I answered honestly. "April, my most recent ex-girlfriend, always said that I tossed, turned and talked in my sleep. Did you get any flak from making your cousin leave yesterday?"

"No. I don't pay attention to family noise, anyway. You guys were gone when I got a chance to leave the kitchen again. How was it?" She looked interested in my answer. It had been a long time since anyone had been interested in my opinion, but then I realized that as a chef, she probably put as much of herself into her food as I did into a painting.

"Honestly?" I asked. She looked a little concerned. "It was one of the best meals I have had in a very long time." I was so glad I could answer that honestly. I was a bad liar.

"Really?" She flashed that crooked smile again. "That's great."

"You're a great chef, at least based on my limited experience with your cooking." I was supposed to ask her about the incident, but I didn't want to do so. I was getting a nice little warm feeling in the pit of my stomach whenever I saw her. Bringing up the incident could ruin that.

"Can I ask you something?" She seemed a little uneasy.

"Okay." Normally I don't allow personal questions. I never know what people are going to ask. Usually, it's about the accident or incident or whatever you want to call it. Sometimes it's about where I get my ideas. I don't have good answers for either line of questioning.

"Were you in love with Gwen?"

"What?" I was so startled I laughed. At least I knew the answer to that question. "No. No I wasn't at all. Why do you ask?"

"It was just one of those things I always wondered about. I mean, after it got around that you came out, I just wondered." She seemed unexpectedly shy.

"Never even crushed on her. That is true. I loved Gwen like a sister. Gabby, on the other hand, I had crushed on her in high school."

"Do you now?"

"No." I smiled this time. "Not at all."

"Oh." She looked down at her mug of coffee. The silence grew between us. It felt like a storm before lightning struck.

"You don't remember a lot of that time period, do you?" I felt as if that was a safe question. After all, I remembered little from when I was nine.

"Not really." She didn't look up from her coffee. "I mean, I have some memories from that time, but not a whole lot. I remember the time after a lot better. Well, not better, but..." I seemed to have broken her, or at least reached a place where she was not comfortable.

"I know." I reached and placed a hand on one of hers. "I do too." That was very true. The time immediately after, I do not remember too clearly. I had very confused memories about a lot the time right before and a couple of years after the incident. Several of those memories I had tried to forget, others were bare images in a faded book. They were ghosts, insubstantial and made of cheap watercolor.

"A lot of my memories about Gwen have you in them, too. It's weird. I remember the others mostly through stories or old newspaper clippings." She shrugged. "It's like watching a newsreel or something our grandparents used to watch."

"Do you still have those clippings?" I asked. She seemed surprised by either the question or of the eagerness with which I asked.

"Maybe. I have a bunch of all that old stuff." She retreated into herself a little. It was strange, she had seemed so open before.

"If you ever feel like sharing, I would love to see some of it." I tried to restrain myself. The last thing I wanted to do was scare her away. I really got the feeling, maybe it was just wishful thinking, that Stephanie had the potential to be more than a friend.

"I live above the restaurant. I have everything there." She seemed subdued. Something had shifted. But I was uncertain what.

"Did I say something?"

"No. It's just." She took a deep breath. "In a very strange way, I feel like I lost two sisters. Only that's not quite that accurate. It just makes me sad, I guess. Even after all this time."

"I get it. I do. I don't remember what happened. I wish I did. In fact, we're trying to remember. It wasn't easy after. I lost friends, families.

A whole community turned its back on us," I admitted. Surprisingly, I didn't feel as if I was complaining.

"It's horrible. It really is." She stood to go. "Come by one night after we close the kitchen at ten. The stairs are around back. I'll show you that stuff. Just text me first so I know to clean up a little."

"Thank you. I'll take you up on that." I promised. I watched her walk out and almost followed until I realized I had not ordered. I was hungry so I waved the server closer and asked for the same breakfast I ordered the day before. It was comforting.

After breakfast, I finished my run by heading back home. I showered and changed clothes. From what firsthand knowledge I had about hospitals, the best time to see Gabby was between breakfast and lunch. The doctors would have already done the first set of rounds and then she should have swatches of time when no one came in to poke or prod her.

I was not sure, but I was pretty sure I was followed. My anxiety started climbing again as the gray sedan behind me turned into the hospital parking lot as well. As soon as I parked, I pulled out my flask and took a long gulp. I watched the car pull into a space a few cars down. I was greatly relieved when I realized an older lady, complete with thin white hair teased and lacquered with hairspray, struggled to climb out of the rear.

I walked inside, trying hard to not look over my shoulder as I did so. I checked my phone, since I couldn't remember what room they had taken Gabby. I didn't find a text from her or her parents with that information.

I walked up to where the volunteers staffed the information desk. I spared a thought about what Gabby would say about unpaid labor from retirees. I shrugged that off and got the lady's attention.

"I'm sorry to bother you, but I'm looking for a patient. Gabriella Rodriguez. She was brought in last night with a stab wound."

"I'll look her up for you." The lady turned to the computer. "Are you a friend or family?"

"Friend." I looked around. The woman who had been following me was standing at the gift shop window. I could feel her looking at me. It wasn't crowded, and most people used one of the other entrances if they knew where they were going, but there were still people around. I could feel their stares.

"There's no one in the hospital by that name, ma'am. Are you sure this is the right hospital?" The lady gave me a look that I could not interpret but made the hairs on the back of my neck stand up.

"No, I saw her here yesterday. I'm sure."

"Was she admitted under a different name?"

"No. There's no reason for that." I stood away from the desk. "Are you sure she's not here?"

"Quite so, ma'am. Perhaps there's a number you can call her or someone else who knows her whereabouts. Unless you've managed to lose another one."

"Pardon me?" Those words were like a glass of cold water thrown on my face. "What?"

"I said perhaps you could call someone else to find out where your friend has been taken."

"Excuse me, ma'am." The woman who followed me stepped up to the counter and got the volunteer's attention. "I'm looking for my nephew. He was brought in this morning."

"Certainly." She smiled at me. "Excuse me, I must see to this woman."

"Yeah, of course." I was confused. I checked my phone again. I could not find any text or anything else telling me what room Gabby was in.

Not knowing what else to do, I went back to my car. I was rather hungry again so I checked the fast-food options. Grabbing lunch seemed as good a thing to do as any.

Before long I had a taco salad and a pretty large burrito. It wasn't until I got back and sat my food on the table that I realized they didn't give me any plastic utensils. I put food in Vinnie's dish and then walked to the house.

Mom had dishes drying in the drain. I grabbed a fork and was about to leave when I noticed the planter in the kitchen window. It was Frohike's dinner dish. She had put his collar around it with the tag in clear view. A small succulent was growing out of it.

That sick feeling in my stomach was back, as was the pain in my head. I made it back to the guest house before I started vomiting. When I could finally breathe again, I crawled to the bed and pulled myself up on to it.

Vinnie joined me, curling behind my knees as I laid in the fetal position, one hand clutched to my head and the other to my stomach. I can't believe I had almost forgotten Frohike.

I felt tears fall and a lump grow in my throat. I remembered saying to Silas that I was a cat person. That hadn't always been true. I had a dog once. Frohike, named for my favorite Lone Gunman, had been a mutt. We figured he was part terrier from the snout, but that was all that was definable. He had been so sweet. He had slept at the end of my bed every night for two years.

I remembered coming home one day my senior year in high school to find my mother in tears. She had found Frohike in her roses. He had been dead, we assumed, for several hours, at least since I had let him out that morning. I had forgotten that, after the accident.

I reached and pulled Vinnie close to me. He allowed himself to be cuddled until I fell asleep.

Chapter Fourteen

I woke early the next morning. I felt like shit. I staggered to the bathroom and looked in the mirror. I looked like shit. My eyes were bloodshot and swollen. My face was pale and bloated.

I was restless and hungry. I pulled on what clothing I found and jogged down to Mabel's for breakfast. At least I knew I could always count on it.

I didn't talk to anyone other than the server long enough to order coffee and breakfast. Someone had left a copy of the newspaper on the counter. I skimmed it, not really taking anything in that I was reading.

I was scared to be recognized. I was scared that I was being followed. My hands shook with tremors I could not control. I snuck some whiskey from the flask in my hoodie to my coffee, hoping it would settle me down.

I ate half of my breakfast and drank two cups of modified coffee. When it didn't help, I paid for my meal and walked back home. I poured a large glass of orange juice and liberally added vodka.

I spent the next several hours researching things on my phone. I hated the smaller screen, but I didn't want to risk looking anything up on my laptop. I didn't trust my parents or their connection to the Internet. Vinnie joined me on the bed as I searched and read.

Someone at the local paper had taken the time and trouble to put all the back issues online and open to the public. I was extremely grateful for that. It allowed me to search through local disappearances in my bed and with copious amounts of alcohol rather than going to the library.

I didn't bother reading through the local coverage of our lost three days. Instead, I looked for others who may have had something similar happen to them. I failed to find anything. I did, however, discover that Twyla had run away from home several times as a child and had spent some time in custody. The local paper published the police reports and a simple search for her name had yielded a lot. However, yielded little else. I had to widen my search.

I had always shied away from conspiracy theories unless you count the JFK stories. I always thought that the majority of them were tinfoil hat level nutters. Just a five-minute search on the Internet had me thinking otherwise. It also had me wrapping my computer in aluminum foil and hiding it. Circumstances and the internet had me freaked. As an added precaution, I turned off everything I could think of in my cell phone that could be tracked. All of this definitely called for alcohol, and I imbibed liberally.

When it grew dark, I went outside and got the backpack. I had found a few old bricks of moderate weight and put them in my backpack to make it feel full if anyone checked. I took the ledger Silas and I had taken from the Hawkins house and stuck it beneath the spare tire in my car's trunk. I felt that was an unlikely place for anyone to look for it. I made sure no one was around when I did it. I couldn't trust anyone. My parents could have been in on it, as well. I was pretty sure the people I used to call friends were. Maybe even Gabby. Especially her. It would have been so easy for them to gaslight me. Hell, Gabby had even shared my bed several times. Was it out of pity or a need to keep everything secret? I didn't know. There were too many possibilities.

It smelled like rain. I pulled on a pair of sneakers and a dark hoodie and began walking. It would be best if no one saw me drive to Stephanie's place. I figured it would be easier to elude watchers if I was on foot. It wasn't far and I had a flask and a half to keep me company on the way.

These flasks had been filled recently. I didn't trust that someone didn't put something in the open bottles I had already. I bought new ones. I washed each flask twice before pouring the new alcohol in them. I was taking no chances. I didn't know who these people were, but I knew what they were capable of. Somewhere in my brain was the truth of what had happened that weekend and some organized agency was making sure it stayed locked away. I wasn't having it anymore.

The roads were quiet as I left my parents' little neighborhood and walked downtown. I think it was a weeknight. I wasn't sure, but the bars were closed. Of course, someone could have planned that to lure me into letting my guard down.

I walked behind the restaurant, trying to stay out of the streetlight as much as possible. There was a set of stairs leading to the second floor. She had said that was where she lived. I crept up them and knocked. I didn't use the doorbell. It could be wired to alert someone else of my presence.

"Who's there?" After five minutes or perhaps ten years, I heard a voice on the other side of the door. "Claire?"

"Can I come in?"

Stephanie stood awkwardly behind the door, her Gwen face looking confused.

"Yeah, sure." She was wearing a fuzzy blue robe. At least I think it was blue. It seemed glow at the edges. "What's going on? Were you supposed to come here tonight? You didn't text or anything."

"I need information. You have it. I need you to give it to me." I barely looked around what was clearly a loft. She steered me to a couch and I'm pretty sure I sat down. It's how I noticed she was so much taller than me.

"Claire, it's late. Do you think maybe we can talk about this some other time?" She kept looking over her shoulder.

"They're watching you, too, aren't they? It's because you know. And you have her face."

"What?" Maybe I was standing, and she was just incredibly tall, because she pushed me down on the couch. Or maybe I stood up and she pushed me back down. It was getting cloudy in the room and everything glittered at the edges.

"You know. You wear her face, and you know. Did she tell you?" It was important to find out. Someone knew. Someone knew everything and it wasn't me.

"You're not making any sense."

"I'm sorry. The people, the whatever, they're watching you." I had to tell her, to make her understand that we were all being watched. They were out there.

"No one is watching me." She backed away a few steps and glanced quickly over her shoulder.

"Why do you keep looking over your shoulder, then?" It was like she purposely didn't want to understand, or to help me understand.

"Because I really don't want to wake up my girlfriend."

"Damn. You have a girlfriend? Shit. Rejected by the same face twice." That didn't seem accurate for some reason. It bothered me. "No. Not twice. Just this once. I was never attracted to you before. We were friends." That seemed true when nothing else did.

"Claire, we weren't friends. You were friends with Gwen. Dylan and I were just the annoying tagalongs. You guys hated us."

"I could never hate you, Gwen. I'm so sorry I couldn't protect you. It's all my fault. You're right to hate me." I put my head in my hands. It wanted to come off and I was tempted to let it.

"Claire, is there someone I should call?" Her hands were cold and enormous, or maybe I was just burning up and really small. I could feel them through my shirt when she put her hands on my shoulders.

"Who do you want to call?" She was leaning in, staring at me. I didn't remember seeing her move.

"No." The voice stopped coming from Gwen's face for a moment and eyes that were not Gwen's looked at me. "Do you have anyone I should call?"

"Ghostbusters? You're haunting me. Is it because I had a crush on Gabby? But you were with Oliver and very straight. And we were best friends, and I never felt that way about you anyway. Did that bother you?"

"Claire, I'm not Gwen. My name is Stephanie. Gwen was my older sister. Do you remember that?"

"You had a brother and a sister, right?" That made sense. I remembered those pesky, annoying dorks. They were always trying to do what we did and would run tell on us if we excluded them.

"Right. You were best friends with my sister. My parents made you two take us trick or treating the Halloween before Gwen disappeared. Do you remember that? You were both in costumes."

"You were wearing a trench coat."

"Gwen went as Scully and you went as Mulder. Do you remember? You wanted me and Tony to go as little green men, but we wouldn't. I went as a basketball player and Tony went as Woody. Does any of this ring a bell?"

"I don't hear bells. I hear static. It's really bad in my left ear. I don't know why. Do you know why?" My brain felt fuzzy. I wanted to sleep. Maybe it was dream and I wanted to wake. I wasn't sure. Everything felt like it was underwater. The lights had halos around them. Everything was giving off an aura field and it made me want to run and hide.

"No. I don't." Her face got really close to me. "Do you have anyone I should call? Is your mom home?"

"You have amazing eyes. I always thought they were blue, but those are like hypnotically green. Not grasshopper green. But nice."

"Can I see your phone?"

"Yeah. I have one of those." I pulled a crinkling package from my pocket.

"Why is this wrapped in aluminum foil? Never mind. What do you call your mother?"

"I don't. She calls me."

"I'll figure it out. Stay there, okay? It's really important that you stay right there." Her face went away. It took the rest of her body with it.

"I can stay." I felt the world titling. I expected a harsh feeling and a thud, but it was soft and nice. It was so warm. I liked it there.

Chapter Fifteen

It was with some surprise that I woke up surrounded by strong, warm arms and muted colors. There was a familiar soreness in the muscles of my right arm. Realizing what it was, I groaned and rolled. I fully expected to find myself in a cold, sterile hospital room, alone and cold, the warmth a result of memory or a fading dream.

"Hey." Gabby's green eyes were hazy, complete with bags. I wondered for a moment how long it had been since she had slept peacefully. "You're back. Feeling okay?"

"What? How?" I struggled to sit up. She let go of me and helped. "What did you give me?"

"You know what I gave you." She rubbed my arm near where the shot must have been. "Just don't ask me where I got it. Or how. I had to call in a few favors and break a few laws since I'm not a Psychiatric Nurse Practitioner."

"What happened?" I was scared to know. I looked around and realized we were in my childhood bedroom. The top of the dresser was littered with prescription pill bottles, a few flasks, and now empty alcohol bottles. "I can't be in here. Dad said I can never sleep under his roof again."

"It's okay." I felt the bed shift. "I'm gonna get us some coffee. Take a moment and let the fog lift, okay? There's a bottle of water and your meds just there. Take that and I'll be back in a few minutes."

"Yeah. Okay."

I looked around the room again. It struck me that while the colors weren't as muted as I had thought, they were more real and less vivid. It was like someone had finally turned off the enhanced filters in Photoshop and I was suddenly seeing the reality underneath. I noticed Vinnie in the window. He was back to his normal gray.

"Fuck." I knew what that meant. I sank back into the pillows as I felt the usual mix of embarrassment and regret swirled in my stomach. How long had I let it go this time? More importantly what was real and what had been an illusion. I always felt like I was caught between two states of being whenever this happened. I guess I was. Is it live or is it Memorex? Every time, that's what it came down to.

"Hey." Gabby carried two steaming mugs of coffee, looking surprisingly well for someone I remembered seeing getting stabbed and almost dying. She handed me a cup and then sat down on the bed and facing me. "I know that look. You're questioning everything right now, aren't you?"

"Yeah. What happened? You were stabbed. Twyla stabbed you at the funeral. What?" I held on to the coffee cup to make sure it was real. It was warm and I could smell the rich aroma. That didn't mean anything, of course. Hallucinations, illusions, delusions, whatever the technical term they were best defined by could fool every sense.

"While that is a good question, it's a little too vague to start with. I guess I can give you a timeline of recent events. However, I need to know for sure. When did you stop taking your medication?" She looked at me, right in the eyes. I searched for any meaning I could find in them, even though I didn't trust my own senses.

"I didn't stop." I couldn't help the lie. I knew she wouldn't believe it and I was right. She barely let me stop talking.

"Don't lie to me, Claire. You did. You stopped. I checked your bottles. The prescriptions were filled two months ago and there's barely a third missing from each bottle. I know you don't reuse bottles. Plus, I checked. You haven't picked up the most recent refills. I had them sent here to the local chain." She finally looked away.

"Gabby, I—" I felt my shame roll through and across me like a storm surge. Maybe I imagined it, it certainly wouldn't be the first time, but I felt as if I could feel her disappointment radiating and filling the room.

"You've been off your meds and drinking since you sold that painting, haven't you?"

"I..." I looked everywhere but at her eyes. I didn't want to see the anger, the disappointment, the reproachfulness there. I looked again at Vinnie and he seemed to be giving me the same look. "Yes. I thought I was okay."

"I get it. You sold the painting. Your demons went quiet for a little while, but they started coming back and you didn't think to get back on your meds or call the therapist you haven't seen in six months, did you? Nope, you crawled inside a bottle and stayed there. You know better than I do that all of that, the doubts, the illness, everything comes back stronger when you do that."

"Yeah, I know, and they did. I just didn't want to admit it." There was more, but I wasn't ready to talk to her about it. Somehow, though, I think she knew. Gabby had always known me better than anyone, even myself.

"Alcohol just makes it worse, babe. You know that." She looked down at her hands. "It's not the time to put you on the path of most destruction. I didn't mean to guilt you. It's just… Claire, when you… I just hate to see you like that. I know you hate it too."

"I do. I really do."

"Okay. Enough with the blaming and shit. What's the only thing you remember? Tell me how you remember everything, and I'll tell you if it happened or not."

"We went to the funeral. Twyla..." I felt panic at the very thought. "You were stabbed, she tried to kill you! I thought you were going to die. Are you okay? How are you okay?"

"I'm, well…I'm not fine. Getting stabbed hurts like a son of a bitch.

Fortunately, it was a short knife and Twyla's an idiotic fucknut. She missed anything vital. She got me a couple of times though, so I had stitches and glue and an MRI. They let me go after they made sure I wasn't going to fall and crack my head open or anything. I did lose some blood, but that was like a week ago. I'm pretty much back to normal. A little sore though and the stitches itch, but that'll go away. Next."

"I snuck into the mental ward to see Twyla." I felt like that had really occurred. It felt a little like a bad action flick, but it did have a sense of authenticity. I ran my hand across my cheek and felt scabs from the scratches she had given me.

"You know we don't call it that anymore, right?"

"I've been a resident. I'll call it what I want." It was a line I had drawn from the beginning. It was the age old I can say it, but you can't think.

"There's my girl." She patted my hand.

"Anyway, Twyla accused me of abandoning Gwen and never caring for her. She kept going on about aliens. That's got to be a delusion, right?"

"For her yes. For you? No. You did go talk to her. You didn't sneak so much as manage to be unthreatening until you woke up Twyla's roommate."

"Shit, I really did that? I have no idea. I guess the helicopters were a delusion. Please tell me they were." I hid my face in her shoulder.

"Yeah. No one is following us. They've been training pilots at the base just like they have every year since it's been open."

"Twyla kept saying it was aliens."

"Yeah, well, Twyla'd set someone's peanut allergies off she's so nutty, batshit crazy." Gabby laughed gently. "What else?"

"Um, Silas and I broke into the Hawkins house. Something chased us out there. I think we were shot at."

"We'll ask Silas about that, but from what he said, y'all didn't find anything. Someone came home early, and you could sneak back out."

"No, that's not how I remember it." I could close my eyes and see that tall, menacing shadow man following me through the trees.

"Claire, sweetheart, you know that delusions often feel like real memories because, for your brain, they were very real. We'll ask him about it again, but I assure you. I wasn't almost killed, we are not being followed, and aliens didn't abduct us."

"I remember walking to see Stephanie about the research her mother had done on our disappearance. I thought I was being followed, so I hid something in my trunk and decided it would be easiest to walk. I don't remember much after that. What happened?" I asked even though a very large part of me didn't want to know. Sometimes the amnesia like holes were a blessing.

"You, ah, went there. You two talked. You collapsed. She called your mom. Your mother called me. I met her here and then we went and got you and brought you back here. We figured out what was going on with you. I did what I could to get you back on your medication."

"How long ago was that?" I pulled my head off her shoulder, scared of the answer.

"Three days. You've been asleep or in some sort of dissociative state for three days."

"Shit. Really?" I looked around the room again. At that moment, I believed her. My head itched, and I suddenly realized my teeth were in a horrible condition.

"We figured it was easier to look after you in here. Your mom said that she's offered to let you stay in the house since your dad left, but you keep refusing." She held up a hand to stop my objections. "I know. I know what he said, but he hasn't lived here in fifteen years. It's not his roof anymore."

"Yeah. That's true. I forgot. I remember thinking it was odd he didn't come out to see me when I got here, but I just figured he was still mad at me. Fuck, I hate this."

"I know you do. I hate it for you." She pulled me into an awkward hug. I rested my chin on her shoulder. "The others will be here in about an hour. Your mom's going to a garden club thing. We're going to order pizza and really talk. You think you feel up to that?"

"I don't know. I feel really raw, but just about every therapist I've ever had has said I need to know what happened. Like if I could find out that she drowned or choked to death on the anchor, I'd feel a sense of closure and I wouldn't be so guilty."

"It's a shame that we still don't understand PTSD, especially long-term PTSD added to survivor's guilt, and all the other shit that happened to you. Goddamn that first doctor and the antipsychotics he put you on!" She got up again. "I'm going to go order the pizza. Why don't you go take a shower? Concentrate on the little things to keep yourself grounded, okay?"

"I can do that. Thanks, Gabby. I don't know what I would do without you."

"You'd survive, Claire, that's what you do."

I had no answer to that. I didn't believe her, and I certainly didn't feel up to an argument about my unsuitableness to survive. Instead, I gathered a change of clothes and went down the hall to the bathroom. Vinnie followed me.

It felt so good to strip off clothes I had been wearing, for I don't know how long, and climb into a warm shower. I wanted to make it as hot as possible, but I remembered at the last moment that I wasn't in my apartment. This house had older pipes and a smaller hot water heater. At least the water pressure was better.

I stood for a long time under that spray and did nothing more than feel it. Finally, when I felt I had been there long enough, I washed. It was like I was washing weeks away instead of days. Since I didn't really know how long I had been in my latest dissociative fugue, I washed my hair twice.

Vinnie sat inside the shower curtain, right at the very edge of the spray, on the rim of the bathtub. That made me feel better. People complain about cats and how aloof they are as a species, but I don't think they've ever had a cat choose them. Vinnie saved me as much as I had saved him as a kitten.

When I finally felt like myself, I turned the water off and got dressed. I debated on makeup for a moment but decided against it. It was my mother's house, so there was no reason for pretentiousness. After everything I had recently been through, my friends could deal. I was considerate enough to put on a bra, though I resented it.

That done, I opened the door, took a deep breath, and walked down the hallway.

Chapter Sixteen

Standing in the hallway, I heard Gabby let them in. I heard the clamor for pizza. Some things never change. I could remember the same fights about pizza on Friday nights so many years ago. My brain was still fuzzy, but I could feel myself returning. I mean, it's not like I went away, or was another person, but when I let that happen, got off my meds and everything, it was like I was a passenger, and I didn't recognize the driver.

I wasn't sure of my reception. I didn't yet remember how off the rails I had gone. These were my friends, but I didn't trust them. I didn't remember who they were as people any more than I remembered who I had been. I squared my shoulders and walked in.

"Claire, I saved you a seat." Zu patted the seat beside her. "Gabby's got your pizza."

"Thanks." I sat gingerly on the sofa beside her. I had always like Zu, I think. She had been one of the few Black kids in band, like Gabby had been the only one of Hispanic descent. She and Gabby had bonded in junior high before the two of them had joined the rest of the group. We had been a group of outcasts in a way, even though Gwen and Oliver were popular and beautiful. At least they could have been, had they not been in the band or interested in anything other than themselves.

"You know, for a long time I thought this thing with you was an act, but you really don't remember, do you?" I didn't like the way Oliver was looking at me. I couldn't tell what he was thinking. Maybe I never had been able to.

"I told you, Oliver. Claire doesn't remember most of the trip. Zu and I remember more, but not one of us has an idea what happened to Gwen." Gabby handed me my plate.

"No. Someone knows." Oliver stood and paced.

"Maybe it was really aliens." Silas threw an arm over the chair and winked at me. I almost choked on my first bite. I quickly lost my appetite. "Gwen's mom certainly seemed to think so."

"How do you know that?" I looked at him closely. I could never seem to tell how much of that indifferent, rich boy persona of his was real.

"I guess the local rumors didn't make it all the way to the state hospital." I resisted the urge to make him regret that lazy smirk.

"Silas, that's not nice. We were gone for so long and Gwen wasn't found with us. You know Oliver and Claire had it harder than we did. Our life certainly wasn't easy after." Zu touched my shoulder briefly.

"Thanks, Zu. It's true though. It's hard to listen to rumors when you're pumped full of antipsychotic cocktails because you can't sleep an hour without waking up screaming from nightmares and you're convinced your dead best friend's ghost is haunting you for revenge, but you have no idea why." They stared at me in silence. I had only ever told Gabby that. My mom knew, because the doctors had told her, but I had only ever told Gabby. She took my hand and squeezed it. For a moment I was lost in memories of being cradled in those arms at night, how she would share her strength with me. "So yes, Silas. It seems I missed those rumors. Please. Enlighten me."

"Well, rumor has it that not long after the memorial service, Ms. Crosby started drinking pretty heavily."

"Silas, buddy, are you sure this is a good time?" Oliver nodded in my direction.

"Claire can take it. She's tough." I gave him a weak smile. "Anyway, it got really bad. Mr. Crosby kicked her out and kept her from seeing the other two kids. Ms. Crosby spent most of her time at Fiona's, that white trash bar out on the highway. Apparently, she became convinced we were abducted by aliens, and they kept Gwen. Before she ran her car into that tree, she stayed with crazy pants' parents. As we all know, that entire family is full of crackpots. I mean, just look at what Fucknuts did to Gabby at the funeral."

"And what she said after." I shook my head at the memory of my visit to her. "And people think I'm crazy."

"Only the best artists are." Gabby squeezed my hand again and smiled a bit. "But you're not really crazy, Claire. You know that." I squeezed back in thanks.

"So, we know it wasn't aliens. They don't exist and even if they did, they wouldn't go around abducting teenagers," Zu said.

"You're letting that pizza get cold. You need to eat." Gabby gently poked me in the ribs. I looked around, but no one seemed to be looking at me. Zu and Oliver were staring at Silas.

"Maybe it was an axe murderer. Or wolves. Or she took the boat and left us there." Silas was still wearing that shitty grin. "I mean, we've been given all sorts of answers. Who wants to choose which one it was?"

"We can't do that. I can't...I need..." I took a deep breath. "I need to know what happened. Can anyone, please, tell me. Really tell me. The truth."

"What the shit, Claire. We've been through this. We went out on the boat and Gwen never came back." Silas put a leg over the arm of the chair and leaned back. "What does it really matter?"

"Matter? It matters. Gwen was my first real girlfriend. She was the first person I loved who wasn't in my family. She had a family. Her disappearance wrecked her family and our lives. If we had answers, it might bring about some sort of healing." Oliver looked more serious than I had ever seen him.

"That was a nice speech, Oliver, but do you honestly believe that?" Zu asked. "I mean you were pretty much suspect number one. If I remember correctly, you claimed some sort of amnesia at the time."

"No, that was Claire." Silas pointed at me. "Bet that hides a lot of guilt. Not that I believe you did anything, of course."

"Can the shit, Silas. Why are you being such an asshole?" Gabby nudged the plate on my lap. I took the hint and took another bite, even though it stuck in my throat.

"I'm sorry, Gabby. How would you like to go about solving a mystery that happened in nineteen ninety-six? You want to contact that cartoon dog and his ill-kempt companions?"

"We should go back to the island." Oliver had his hands in his hair, pacing the length of the room.

"What? Are you all nuts?" Zu threw her hands in the air.

"Nope, just me." I placed my plate on the coffee table. "I'm up for it."

"Claire, you can't possibly..." Gabby leaned forward and placed a hand on my knee.

"That is absolutely ridiculous." Zu looked around at me. It was the first time I could see her question my sanity.

"Zu, Gabby, guys, thanks. I need to know. It's wrecked my life for so long. Maybe it'll help. One of my many, many therapists always tried to hypnotize me to take me back to that trip. It never worked. He thought I had a mental block around it. Several of them thought that. Something about dissociative amnesia and PTSD."

"Guess that means Silas needs to call his dad and ask for the boat keys, if he'd lend them to us again." Oliver sat down. "Claire, does your mother keep any beer here?"

"No, she doesn't." Gabby answered before I could. I knew what that meant. I was back on the wagon. I was sure they had already poured out every bit of hidden alcohol.

"Mom's not a big drinker." I felt certain that was true. I couldn't remember my mom ever having more than a glass of wine and even that was rare.

"Whatever, I can wait. So, are we going to go? Silas, *can* you get your dad's boat?" Oliver wiped his hands on his pants.

"Of course." Silas scoffed. "I still take whichever boat out I want."

"Spoiled little rich boy." I'm not sure Zu meant for anyone to hear her, but I did. "Why did I ever think he was fuckable?"

"Silas." I had a lot of practice at not laughing. It was something that worked well when I had been in treatment. "When can we go?"

"Tomorrow, if you still want to. I mean, I think it's kinda pointless. There's not going to be any clues or fuck-all after twenty-plus years and a few hurricanes."

"Maybe Claire's right, though. Maybe we just need to be in similar surroundings for it to spark something." Zu stood. She placed her plate on the coffee table and walked to the window. "At least this time we'll have a better idea what the weather will be like. It's gotten a lot more accurate in recent years."

"That storm did come out of nowhere," Oliver said.

"Storm?" I asked. It tickled at the edge of my memory. "We were on the island and a storm came through."

"Yeah, a storm. Knocked a few tents down, blew up some deadfall, maybe made the boat lose the anchor." Silas waved his hand around. "Big fucking deal, man. But if you want to go, we'll go. I'll check the weather, get the boat filled up, and text everyone a time to meet. Sound good?"

"Yes. Do we need to bring anything?" Gabby asked. "It's been a while since I was on a boat, but if I remember right, we'll want drinks and snacks."

"A whole picnic maybe." Zu sat back down. "Are we camping again?"

"Why not?" Silas twirled his hand again. "What's that saying? In for a penny?"

"Then we'll split the refreshments." I reached and got a pad and pen my mother had left by her chair, a habit from when she had a home phone. "Who wants to get what?"

"I don't think we'll need a list." Gabby took the pad and pen from my hand. "I'll get drinks, water and soda."

"The boat we're gonna use has ice chests already on it. I will get ice when I get the gas for it."

"I'll get chips and breakfast stuff," Zu volunteered.

"I suppose I can get a sandwich tray and stuff." Oliver shrugged.

"That doesn't leave me anything to get."

"You can come with me to get drinks. We'll pick up whatever else we can think of while we're at the store," Gabby said.

"Okay, that works." I gave in. Their brains were working better than mine was. I was content to let them plan. Gabby, at least, I trusted. She had always been practical.

"Since we've gotten that sorted out, I'm getting out of here." Silas stood. "I'll text everyone in the morning."

"Okay. See you then." Oliver stepped aside and let Silas open the door.

"You're not leaving on my account, are you?" my mother asked as she stepped inside.

"Ms. Evans. I didn't see you there." Silas was back in his charming mode. "Of course, I'm not leaving on your account. Had I known you'd be returning, I would have prolonged my stay."

"Charmer." I saw her eyes dart around the room. "Sorry to interrupt."

"We were just finishing up." Zu stood and began gathering the plates. Oliver grabbed the glasses.

"It's okay, leave that. I'll clean up in a few minutes." Mom put her purse on the table by the door. "Before I go change, anything I can get any of you?"

"No thank you." Oliver grabbed his jacket off the back of the chair. "I'm going to head out, as well. Thank you, Ms. Evans. Your hospitality is always amazing."

"You know, I think I'll follow you out. Dad gets a bit testy if someone wakes him up after he's fallen asleep in front of the TV." Zu reached down and patted my shoulder. "I'll see you tomorrow."

"Yeah. Yeah, we'll see everyone tomorrow." It felt different when my mom entered the house. It was like she was interrupting us as teenagers again. I felt awkward and ungainly. "Do you mind if I go back to my room?"

"No, go ahead." Mom waved me away. "Go see that your cat hasn't destroyed my curtains."

"He's a good kitty. He has never torn up curtains."

"That's because you have blinds," Gabby said. "Go see to Vinnie. I'll help your mother clean up."

"I'm going to get comfortable first. I hope I won't embarrass you, Gabriella, if I come out in my pajamas."

"No, ma'am. It's your house, you should be comfortable."

"I am going to take this damn bra off," I called behind me. Let them clean up the living room because I was tired and prickly.

Chapter Seventeen

It was strange being back in my childhood bedroom. Not much had changed since my senior year. It was almost a shrine and that made it very depressing. I opened the closet and realized my entire high school wardrobe was in there, not that I could fit into any of it. Vinnie was curled on a pillow with one paw on his eyes.

"You can clean it out and update everything, if you want." My mom stood just outside the door. She had changed into her pajamas. "I know it can be a bit triggering to be back in here. May I come in?"

"Yeah. It is strange being in here. I remember Dad saying so clearly that I wasn't to spend the night under his roof again. It's like he told me that yesterday."

"There's a lot, it seems, you don't remember. I wish I could help you with that. There are memories I wish I could take away. That's one of them." She sat down on the bed and looked at the floor.

"I probably know this, but where is he?" I leaned against the dresser and crossed my arms. I was quickly learning what Sleeping Beauty must have felt when she woke up to find everything changed. And that everything she remembered was just dreams. It sucked.

"After you kept having nightmares and couldn't go back to school, we let you drop out. You remember that?"

"Vaguely."

"Your father thought you were faking, initially, but your behavior and other influences convinced him to seek more counseling."

"You guys fought about that, didn't you?"

"We fought about a lot of things, Claire."

I stopped and looked at her. "When we were at the wake for Mr. Hawkins, I remembered something. I remembered being upset at school. You and dad had been fighting about something, that part is still unclear, but I remembered that. A few other things, but mainly how uncertain I felt and how kind Mr. Hawkins was to me. I can't rectify that with how he became this big shadowy monster in my head."

"We did argue a lot, your dad and me. We were on a fast train to divorce before your lost weekend." She sighed and reached out for me. I met her halfway. She took my hand in her own. "I need you to know this, Claire. Nothing that happened between me and your father was your fault."

"Something tells me we've had this discussion before."

"We have. I filed for divorce when your father was convinced to have you committed the first time. It was the final straw, but it wasn't the root cause. I don't even know where your father is now. I do know you haven't seen him since then. I haven't seen him since the finalized divorce and he came back to get some of his stuff. Do you have memories of him visiting you?"

"I don't know." I let go of her hand and sat beside her on the bed. "Everything is still so jumbled. I remember this feeling, the clarity I hope it lasts this time."

"That's going to depend on you mostly, but you'll have help. If you let me, I'll be there every step of the way. You could even move back, if you want. Vinnie and I would be here to keep you company and keep you grounded."

"I'll be here, too, as much as I can be, of course." Gabby leaned against the door frame, her ankles crossed and one hand in her pocket. "I'm sorry to interrupt. I put all the leftovers away and was about to head out. I just came in to see if you wanted me to pick you up tomorrow, Claire?"

"I would appreciate it. I don't feel much like driving."

"I wouldn't recommend it." She ran a hand through her short, spiky hair. "I'll borrow mom's car. As much as I hate cars, this place has no public transport, and I don't have my bike with me."

"But the vertigo?" I paused for a moment before a memory returned. "Damn. You bike everywhere because of the carbon footprint thing. How did I get all confused with this conspiracy thing?"

"Well, I do hate flying and I don't drive if I can help it, so you're right about that. I'm not sure why you're all confused on that topic."

"I'll let you two talk." My mom got up and walked out but not before whispering something to Gabby. "I'll be in the living room if you need me, Claire."

"Thanks, mom." I waited until Gabby sat next to me on the bed. It felt as if nothing I had ever known was true. Nothing was the way it seemed. I didn't suffer from dissociative identity disorder, though at one time I had been treated for it. But I felt as if I had suddenly awakened and discovered that someone else had lived my life for the past thirty years or so. Or maybe I had taken someone else's life. I really wasn't sure about much.

"What else do you want to know?"

"I owe Ms. Hawkins an apology, don't I?" I wasn't sure why I blamed Mr. Hawkins for anything, but it feels wrong. "Him too."

"Yeah, maybe. I don't know." She stood and stretched. "Listen, get some sleep. Drink some water. Cuddle Vinnie. Don't try to disappear, but don't beat yourself up about everything either. This time we'll work it out, okay?"

"You think so? I can't keep doing this to you, Mom, me." I felt so small and so toxic, like I was slowly poisoning everyone around me. I hated it.

"It's going to get better, Claire. You're gonna get better." She leaned and kissed the top of my head. It felt like a promise, and that made it all the more reassuring. "I'll see you tomorrow. Get some rest, okay?"

"I will. Thanks, Gabby."

I heard her walk back down the hallway, say something to my

mother in a voice too low for me to hear and close the front door behind her. I moved Vinnie off my pillow, the scamp had not moved, and put him on my lap. He started purring. The vibrations soothed me. I blew out a breath slowly and tried to relax.

Something shattered in the kitchen. Vinnie freaked out, jumped off my lap, and ran under the bed. I was halfway to my door when I heard my mother call out and telling me not to worry. She had knocked a plate off the counter.

I let her deal with it as I got down on my knees and prepared to pull Vinnie out from under the bed. He was wedged between the bed and the wall. His eyes were huge. I began crawling underneath the bed to get him. Normally I would leave him to come out on his own, but he wasn't used to this place yet.

I was expecting him to hiss and back farther into the corner, but he didn't. It was as I was pulling him back and crawling out from under the bed that I nearly jumped out of my skin when I felt something hit my back.

I got Vinnie back on the bed and went back to see what had fallen on me. It was a book. I pulled it out and brought it into the bed with me.

"Well, Vinnie, what do we have here?" I turned it and paused. "Holy shit! I forgot I had this. Why did I hide it?"

It was my final yearbook, the one from my senior year. I flipped it open. There were no signatures. That made sense. I had not been enrolled in school when they had handed them out.

I flipped through it, looking through the portraits of my classmates. I saw Gwen's first. She had the ugly black drape they made all the girls wear then.. Her shoulder-length blonde hair seemed to shimmer even in the picture. Her eyes were bright, her smile hopeful. I had not seen her like that in so long. Every time I remembered her was from a hallucination and she had been pale, wet, wan, and bloodied.

I looked away and saw where Silas's picture should have been. At some point, and I had no memory of this, I or someone had colored on his picture, defacing it with devil horns and a porn star level mustache.

Written across his name was the word liar in bold letters. It was my handwriting.

I flipped through to find the others. I wanted to see if I had done the same to any other pictures. I had not. Oliver was as handsome as ever. Zu's hair was straight and fell around her head in an appealing manner. It was long before she started wearing her hair natural. Gabby's picture was boarded by hearts. I had to shake my head at that. Of course, I had been half in love with her then. Hell, I was still half in love with her, maybe more.

It was my picture that caught my attention. I had avoided looking at it until I had seen the others. I was wearing the same drape as everyone else. The background was the same blue everyone else had. But I was smiling. My eyes were clear. I looked so young and innocent it was hard to believe it was me. Hell, I looked happy.

"Claire, I was going to make a cup of hot chocolate. Would you like one?" My mom tapped on the door. I hadn't closed it completely. It eased open.

"Mom, how did I get this?" I held up the book for her to see the cover.

"Didn't you read the inscription? Mr. Hawkins got yours and brought it to you. It was right before you were admitted the first time."

"I have no memory of that." I flipped back to the very first page. There was a neat line of blue ink I hadn't noticed.

"What's it say? I don't remember. In fact, I have not seen that since he brought it to you."

"It says 'Let me know if you need anything. I'm always here for you. Hopefully, you will remember the rest of your time at Bayview High with fondness.' And then he signed it."

"I never did figure out how you convinced yourself, or let yourself be convinced, of his villainy. He was always looking out for you kids."

"I remember, vaguely, of getting sick in the band hall one day. You and dad were fighting. I was nervous about taking the ACTs and I was worried that if you found out about my crush on Gabby that you'd kick me out. Hawkins followed me into the bathroom and helped me clean myself up a little. I think he checked me out of school and let me go home." I was describing it to her as it came to me.

"He was on your sign out list, so he probably did." She shrugged. "Do they still allow teachers to sign kids out? Guess it doesn't matter. Go on."

"But I remember before I went home that he took me into his office and talked to me. He got me calmed. I think I came out to him. I told him about my fierce love for Gillian Anderson. He was a fan of the show, too."

"He would have been supportive. He was a good man. Every time I would see him or Sylvia out, they would ask about you."

"Do you—" I stopped. What was I going to ask? Did she love and support me? I knew she did, at least when I was thinking straight.

I had been flipping through the pages and came to the section of the yearbook dedicated to random pictures taken throughout the school year. There was a small of one of me, Gwen, and Mr. Hawkins. It must have been taken around Halloween. Gwen and I were dressed as Scully and Mulder complete with ID badges. Hawkins was in a suit and tie. He looked just like the main bad guy from the TV show.

"Mom, can you take me to the hospital tomorrow morning? I think I'd like to see Ms. Hawkins."

"Aren't you supposed to go on the boat tomorrow? I know, Claire, you're gonna do what you want, but I'm not sure that's such a good idea."

"I know. It might not be, but I have to know." I flipped back to Silas's senior portrait. "Do you know why I would have done this?"

"I don't. I know you two broke up but remained friends. He got a bit strange but seemed to accept it after a few weeks. I'll be honest, he worried me there for a little while. But he was very concerned after the accident and talked to your father a lot, went to visit you, gave the doctors some background. I always found that a little odd, but he swore he was just doing it for your benefit. He charmed everyone. Don't you remember any of that?"

"No. A lot of that time is a blur." I rubbed my head and then yawned. "I'm sorry, Mom. I'm worn out. I've had way too much to think about today and it's not going to stop soon."

"I'll let you get to sleep. We'll go see Ms. Hawkins in the morning." She rose and then leaned and kissed the top of my head. "I love you, Claire. Goodnight."

"Thanks, Mom. I love you too."

After she left the room, I flipped back to Gwen's picture, to fix it in my memory again. I needed to be able to see her young and alive. Silas's defaced portrait caught my eyes instead. There was a lot of anger in the markings and drawings on his face. Then there was the word liar over his name.

I had a puzzle that was left from when I was seventeen. I was tired. My mental state was still shaky and I wanted a drink but knew it would be so very harmful. I knew from previous experiences that I had a decision to make. I actually had two. The first decision was to get well. I knew it was going to be tough, but I was resolved to do that. The second was to find out who or what killed Gwen. Maybe they weren't, but they seemed linked. Regardless, I had decided to do both.

With my mind made up, I was able to fall asleep, curled around Vinnie as usual.

Chapter Eighteen

I slept fairly well that night. I woke to the smell of coffee and bacon. It was marvelous. I realized a part of me missed living with someone else. Even if that someone was my mother, it was nice to wake up know there was another person in the house.

I got up and did my morning routine, brushed my teeth, washed my face, changed Vinnie's litter box, before going into the kitchen. It smelled amazing. Vinnie was practically walking on my feet. I got the feeling my mother had been spoiling him. I was proven correct when I saw him race to his food bowl and scraps of bacon and eggs laying on top of his kibble.

"You still want to go to the hospital today?"

"Yes ma'am. If you're okay with that." I sat down at the table. She placed a plate of bacon, scrambled eggs, and toast in front of me.

"Yeah, I have no problem taking you up there. I was going to go up there soon, anyway. Barbara said that they'll be keeping Sylvia up there for a few more days." I had forgotten Ms. Hawkins was part of her gardening club.

"What happened to her? I vaguely remember she collapsed at the funeral."

"She did. I was there, but you all hung around the back." She sat down opposite me with her own plate. "Barbara said that Sylvia had a stroke. She's awake and coherent. Her balance is off, and she's lost some feeling in her right side."

"God, that sucks." I felt a little guilty. It must have shown on my face.

"It's not your fault, Claire." Mom patted my hand. "Strokes happen. Now finish your breakfast and we'll go up to the hospital."

"Yes, ma'am."

After breakfast, I went back to my room and got ready. It didn't take long. I skipped most of my normal makeup routine since I would go out on the boat later. When there was no text from Silas telling me when to meet them, I figured he was still asleep. Instead of bothering Gabby, I wrote an email to Lane. I valued Lane's friendship more than his partnership in the graphic novels. I apologized and gave him a summary of what was going on. Outside of Gabby, Lane was my closest friend. There were people I hung out with in St. Louis, but on this side of my meltdown, they didn't seem to matter too much.

That led me to another realization. Perhaps living in St. Louis by myself wasn't ideal. It never had been. It's not like I needed someone to take care of me, I knew that. Well, maybe I did, but in the way that I needed to be responsible to someone other than myself. I didn't need a babysitter. I needed a support team. Perhaps it would be in my best interest to move home. If nothing else, it gave me one more thing to think about when I already had so many.

"You ready?" Mom tapped on my doorframe.

"Yeah."

The ride to the hospital was quiet. It gave me a chance to observe my mother. I had not noticed before how her hair had gone completely gray or how her face, angular like mine, was wrinkled around the eyes and mouth. I felt as if I was looking at a self-portrait aged twenty-seven years. I was okay with that. My mother was still a good-looking woman.

We parked in front of the hospital near the main entrance. I hoped I would not encounter anyone I had seen on my past visit to the hospital. I remembered that clearly. However, we didn't have to stop and ask anyone anything. Mom already knew where to go.

Ms. Hawkins was on the third floor. I followed Mom through the tiled hallways and into the old elevators. She seemed content to walk in silence. I was fine with that. Now that my brain was regulating itself, silence wasn't such a big deal. Of course, it was hardly silent. Our footsteps echoed on the tile and there were the normal noises of hospital activity.

"Sylvia?" Mom poked her head around the half open the door. "Are you ready for company?"

"Margery, yes please. Come in." Her voice was a bit slurred. "Claire? Oh! It's good to see you."

"Ms. Hawkins." I looked at her closely. She was extremely pale. Her salt and pepper hair fanned out on the pillow beneath her. It made a strange sort of halo around her face. The right half of her mouth and the eye on that side seemed to slant a little downwards.

"I know. I've looked better." Ms. Hawkins smiled, well, half of her mouth raised anyway.

"You look fine, Sylvia. My daughter is just a little cloudy still. She's had a very rough time. As have you, of course." Mom walked fully inside and sat down on the room's only chair.

"I'm sorry, Ms. Hawkins. I still don't remember a lot, but Mr. Hawkins, he was a good man. I do remember that."

"Thank you, Claire. He was closer to some students than others, naturally, but there wasn't a person who walked through his band hall that he didn't care for deeply." She licked her lips. I took the cup off the tray near her bed and offered it to her. She fumbled for a minute with the straw but could drink a little water.

"I have a vague memory of him visiting me. Is that right?" I didn't look at my mother. She would object to my questioning. I wished Gabby was there with me. At least I could get some idea if what I wanted to know would only hurt Ms. Hawkins. "I don't want to push. You don't have to answer. I'm sorry."

"Don't be sorry, Claire. I look much more fragile than I am. I can't answer all your questions, but I can this one." She still looked pale, but there was some fire in her eyes. "He did visit you. At first, we both did. He kept going until your doctor said it was counterproductive."

"I'm sure there's more that Claire wants to talk to you about, but this may not be the best time, Sylvia." Mom stood and walked a little closer to the bed. "The garden ladies and I will come back later. Barbara said something about helping you clean up a bit. We need to get some flowers for your room. It'd cheer things up a bit."

"Perhaps you're right. Claire, you know we both loved you. Robert was so proud when you confided in him. You know that he took several courses in counseling. I think that helped him a lot as a teacher."

"I think it did, as well. He was such a positive influence on so many people. My memories are not trustworthy, but I know that. Hopefully one day I will remember, and his memory will be a blessing." I felt my phone buzz in my pocket. I pulled it out and glanced at the screen. "If you'll excuse me a moment, I need to see what this is."

"Go ahead. I'll say my goodbyes and meet you outside." Mom took the cup from the tray and offered it to Ms. Hawkins.

"When I'm allowed to go home, you come, Claire. We'll have a long talk then, okay?"

"Yes, ma'am." I stepped outside and checked my texts. There was one from Silas. A group text telling us the time to meet him at the dock. I called Gabby.

"Hey, what's up?"

"I just got Silas's text. We still have a few hours before we're supposed to meet him at the dock. Do you want my mom, to drop me off at your house?"

"Are you not at home?"

"No. She brought me up to the hospital to see Ms. Hawkins." I wasn't ready to tell her about the yearbook or anything I had remembered, however faulty, on the phone. In fact, I wasn't sure that I wanted to discuss it yet. "You're not far from here. I can get her to drop me off there."

"Nah, it might be better to meet at that grocery store across the street. We can get lunch at the Chinese place." She laughed. "Unless you think you're going to get seasick."

"I have no idea, but at least noodles would be easy to come back up." I smiled as my mother exited Ms. Hawkins's room. "Mom, can you drop me off at the grocery store across the street? Gabby's gonna meet me there."

"Do you have stuff to go out on the boat? I mean, you didn't pack anything."

"I can bring you stuff. I heard the question," Gabby said. "I can leave in about five minutes. It's less than that to the grocery."

"Okay. That sounds good. I'll see you in a few." I disconnected the call and put the phone back in my pocket. "Gabby's gonna bring some stuff for me to wear."

"She's five inches shorter than you."

"I didn't think about that. I'm sure it'll be okay. If nothing else, we can stop by a store. It's not like I packed anything appropriate for a boat ride, anyway."

"Okay. Let's go then." She waited until we got back in the elevator to speak again. "When are you going back to St. Louis?"

"I don't know. I'm not sure that's a good idea. Why?"

"Well, Dr. Kamaal is supposed to be the best psychiatrist in the state. He teaches classes at the university and sees patients, too."

"And you think I should see him?"

"I do, yes."

"You didn't make an appointment for me already, did you?" I glanced at her as we walked outside the building. She looked straight ahead.

"No, I didn't. I just mentioned it in case you wanted to see him. I mean, he's the best."

"We'll talk about it more when I get home tomorrow, okay?" I wasn't sure what I was supposed to do now. I didn't know if she wanted me to ask to move home or if she wanted to ask me. Then there was the chance she didn't want to share the house with her grown daughter, who suffered from mental health issues. "You'll take care of Vinnie for me?"

"Of course. That one eared cat of yours is quite charming."

"I noticed you gave him bacon."

"A little bacon is not going to hurt him."

"Just make sure it's only a little bacon." I laughed. "He's my baby."

"I know. Do you want me to wait here for Gabby?"

"No, but thank you, Mom. I appreciate it. I'll go in and get started on stuff for the trip."

"Claire, you're my daughter. I love you. Thanks aren't needed." She pulled in front of the store and stopped the car. "Have fun. I hope it's productive. But please, be careful and come home, okay?"

"Okay. I will." I opened the car door and grabbed my bag. "I love you, too. I'll see you tomorrow."

Chapter Nineteen

It had been a long time since I had been in Bayview's local grocery store. They had expanded into another store after the neighboring store closed. It was bright and cheerfully colored. It smelled nice, as well. The air was full, with the smell of fresh produce and cooking food. They had a very popular deli and catered for a lot of local events.

I picked up a sales paper from the stand right inside the automatic doors and flipped through it. I was astonished that the prices were not that different from the local market I frequented in St. Louis. Apparently, the results of a few destructive hurricanes and an oil spill or two wrecked the cost of living.

"Been here long?" Gabby asked as she touched my arm.

"Not really. Just comparing prices between here and there." I put the sales paper back on the stand. "You know what we're here to get?"

"Drinks and anything else we can think of for the trip. I'm sure the others will forget to get vegan."

"I'm not sure they'll have many vegan choices here." I looked around the store. "But I think there's a health food store downtown."

"Eh, probably some overpriced hipster place." She rolled her eyes. "Get a cart. I've been negotiating my way through regular grocery stores. I've got this."

"You know my mother brought up a good point earlier. You're a bit shorter than I am and I know for a fact I'm not going to be able to fit into your clothes. What exactly did you pack for me?" I asked as Gabby inspected a bunch of grapes before placing them in the cart.

"I am aware of the differences in our height. Very aware." She laughed. "However, you're about the same size as my sister-in-law. She and my brother Eduardo are always using Mom's washing machine, so I just borrowed some of her stuff."

"I haven't seen Eduardo and Viv in years. What if we don't have the same taste in clothes? If I remember, she was a bit wilder than I ever was."

"It's not going to matter. It's a boat. We're going to be camping on an island. No one is going to wear designer clothes. Well, Silas might, but he still has a bit of douche about him."

"I know, I'm just..." I shrugged even though she couldn't see me since she was judging bananas.

"Worrying about the little things so you don't have to think about the big ones?" She put the bananas she had chosen beside the grapes. "Too bad it's too early for watermelon."

"You plan on existing on fruit while we're there?"

"Well, it'll help keep everyone hydrated. Besides, I know there's no animal products in grapes."

"Speaking of animal products, you said something about the Chinese place for lunch. How do you know they have vegan stuff? I mean, sure they'll have vegetarian stuff, but vegan?"

"Simple. Aye's parents own the place. She's been vegan since junior high. Well, really, she went vegetarian, and then all the way to vegan by the time we were sophomores. She made them put special stuff on the menu for her, so when she comes home, she can eat there."

"That makes sense. What are we getting now?" Gabby oversaw the cart and groceries. My job was to ask stupid questions. I was good at that.

"Well, we'll probably have a fire, so I was going to see if they have vegan marshmallows. I'm not holding my breath, but it's worth a look."

"S'mores?" My mouth watered. "If they don't have vegan ones, can I still get the regular ones?"

"Claire." She stopped the cart and waited until I noticed. "Have I ever made you, with the exception of making an occasional meat free dinner, ever made you follow my lifestyle?"

"No, you haven't." I did remember a foul green smoothie that had kale and other disgusting leafy things in it, but I didn't remember Gabby ever forcing me to conform to her diet. "Forget I asked."

"You're a goober. It's a good thing I like you." She smiled. It felt good to hear her joke.

"You're a goober, goober." Okay. I wasn't the best at joking back. I was out of practice. "So, water, sports drinks, and sodas. I'm not buying any beer. If Oliver or Silas want any, they'll have to get it themselves."

"Good. Proud of you."

"Thanks." I put two cases of regular soda in the cart as Gabby loaded up on water. "What are we going to do if we can't get any answers?"

"We'll worry about that later. Try to focus on one step at a time, okay?"

"Okay." It was hard. "How many more days do you have off?"

"Two. I have to head back the day after tomorrow to report for duty that night."

"Damn, Gabby. I'm sorry."

"For what? It's not your fault. Let's get the rest of the stuff and then go eat. I'm getting hungry."

"You wanna pick up something like tofu dogs or something?"

"Tofu dogs? Are you teasing me or are you serious?" She squinted at me.

"Well, if we can't find vegan marshmallows, what do you plan on roasting above the fire?"

"Claire, while meatless brats might sound like a good idea, they're completely bland and I doubt we're going to have the ability for me to season it." She turned the cart back toward the fresh fruit and vegetables. "That does give me a good idea, though. I like roasted peppers. They're good on a stick. While I get those, try to find some sticks. I don't want to scrounge for some when we get out there.”

“Okay. Where would I find those?” I stopped for a moment. “Never mind. I think I know. Where shall I meet you?”

“It’s not that big a store. I’ll find you.” She laughed and turned away.

I wandered around until I found the marshmallows. Of course, they didn’t have vegan ones. I didn’t see kabob sticks or anything else we could use to roast things on a fire. However, like most grocery stores, this one had an aisle of general goods for the household. It included stuff like charcoal, lighter fluid, baking pans and so forth. I grabbed a box of aluminum foil and found the sticks.

“I found hotdogs. Not for you, but for me.” Gabby’s smile was broad and happy. “Marshmallows?”

“No. They didn’t have any. In fact, they didn’t seem to have a lot of the common brands either.” I tossed the stuff I had picked up into the cart.

“We’ll stop at a gas station on our way there and get cold drinks. I’m sure the guys haven’t thought about that.”

“Probably not. Are we ready to check out?”

“Yeah, I think so.” She reached into her bag and pulled out a reusable shopping bag.

“You know, your dedication is admirable. Have you always been vegan?”

“Your mind is still full of holes, isn’t it?”

“It is, yes.” I reached into my purse and I pulled out my wallet. The pill box rattle was a little jarring. I wasn’t used to it anymore. “I’ll get this. Now that I’m not going to spend so much money on alcohol, I have a little excess.”

“You’re not mad about all that, are you?” Gabby placed things from the cart onto the conveyor belt. “Never mind. Don’t think about it now. We’ll talk later. Let’s just enjoy this before we get on the boat. I don’t want you to stress.”

“Okay.” I was content merely to exist.

The tremors in my hands were lessening, but the headache was always on the horizon. I was raw, still wounded and knitting myself back together. Gabby's presence had never been threatening. It was not now. I wasn't sure of how well I would hold up around the others, much less on a boat headed back to the site that had helped set off whatever was wrong with my brain. I was grateful I had been pretty much unconscious for three days or so. Hopefully, I had missed the worst of the withdrawals.

We walked out and put the stuff we had bought in Gabby's mother's car and then walked to the Chinese restaurant. I had not eaten there in decades and even then, only once or twice. That was good. There were no emotional memories tied up there. It wasn't a place we went to hang out and my father had not liked Chinese food.

"Two?" an elderly lady greeted us when we walked inside.

"Yes, please." I let Gabby take the lead.

"You can sit anywhere. Someone will be with you in a moment."

"Thank you."

I followed Gabby to a small table for two on the wall of the restaurant. The table was square, with two black lacquered chairs on either side. I smiled. The table was right beneath a mural of the Great Wall of China.

"I thought Aye was Vietnamese?"

"She is. But when her grandparents got here, they didn't think a Vietnamese restaurant would be well received. So, they opened this place. I think during the years they've been incorporating more Vietnamese cuisine." She pulled a menu from the holder on the table. "In fact, the vegan pho is incredible."

"I think I'll stick to General Tso's chicken." I looked at the menu. "Or Mongolian Beef. That sounds pretty good."

"I'm glad to see your interest in food is back."

"Well, I need some way to pack on the pounds since I won't be drinking anymore." I resisted the urge to roll my eyes. "I suppose I should find a twelve-step program."

"It would be a good idea." Gabby licked her lips. It was her tell.

She was about to approach a topic and she wasn't sure how I would react to it.

"Spill it."

"I know I told you to concentrate on going step by step, but I'm here to help you find a new therapist, if you want me to."

"Thanks." We paused for a moment to order. Gabby got the pho and I ended up with the Mongolian Beef. "Mom mentioned a Dr. Kamaal who is local."

"That would mean staying here. Are you thinking about it?"

"I don't know. Maybe." I shrugged. "Can we talk about something else?"

"Certainly. My stepsister is pregnant again. George is not happy about it."

"Why? He doesn't want to be a grandfather again?"

"It's not that. It's that she's still married, and her husband is deployed. He wasn't here to get her pregnant."

"Oh shit! Yeah, I guess George wouldn't be happy. What's your mom think?" It was nice, gossiping about family affairs.

By the time we were finishing lunch, Silas was texting directions and instructions. We paid and walked back to the car. We still had to stop by a gas station, but we were almost ready to go.

Chapter Twenty

It had been a long time since I had been on a boat. I had tried once, ten years or so ago, to go canoeing with a girlfriend. The anxiety and panic that had caused had led me to a nice two-day stint in a local hospital. It was, of course, the end of another relationship.

The wind whipped at my hair, causing some to break free from the hair tie. It felt good to be sitting there on the bow, letting the way the boat cut through the waves soothe me in a way nothing else had for a very long time. Perhaps it was the medication I was on, but I didn't feel the least bit anxious, at least not about being on the boat itself. Hopefully, I would remember all this trip unlike the past, disastrous one.

"How are you holding up?" Gabby pulled her sunglasses off and stuck them in the neck of her shirt.

"I'm okay. A bit shaken, I guess."

"Did you take your meds today?"

"Yes, I did. I even brought a few extra, just in case. I don't want to get anywhere near that level of paranoid again." We crested a particularly sharp and choppy set of waves. I bumped into her. She placed a hand on my thigh and squeezed lightly.

"You will regain your sea legs, but it's gonna feel weird until you do. Just remember not to fight the movement and keep your balance centered on your hips."

"I remember. It's just been so long."

"It's been a long time for a lot of things."

"I'm sorry." I wasn't sure she heard me at first. The wind, the waves breaking on the bow, the roar of the engine, it all seemed so loud.

"What are you sorry for?" She turned to face me, and I caught her gaze. I felt that tug behind my navel when I looked into those dancing green eyes. Damn.

"For, uh..." My mouth had suddenly gone dry and the words I had been about to speak evaporated. "For being slap ass nuts and paranoid as hell."

"Claire, you're not nuts." She slid a little closer and put an arm around my shoulders. "I'm honestly surprised you aren't after everything they did to you, but you're not crazy. Not really."

"You're saying it's all in my head?"

"No, I mean you have a real..." She stopped. "Are you teasing me?"

"Yeah." I leaned back on my elbows. "You know, the world looks pretty when you're looking at it through polarized lenses."

"Maybe you should paint it that way."

"Hey girls, what's up?" Oliver joined us on the bow. "This boat is a lot different than the other one. I don't think it's gonna get us as close to the island as the last one did."

"What did the other one look like?" I asked. I had no idea, no memory, of the other boat's layout.

"It was a center console. It didn't have a cabin. This one does," Oliver said. "In fact, and forgive me, it's been a while, but I think the other one was only seventeen feet. This one is thirty-two. Zu's below dealing with the food. She snarled a bit at the tofu dogs or whatever."

"Of course, she did." Gabby laughed. "How long before we get there? Did Silas tell you?"

"About an hour. I was going to ask if you had sunscreen. The breeze can feel cool, and it's still a way from summer, but you can still get sunburned."

"Thanks, Oliver, but we're good," she said.

"I'm sorry. I didn't mean to come across as the all-knowing white male, but I didn't know if anyone would think to remind Claire. I don't know how much you've forgotten."

"Thanks, Oliver. I appreciate that. Zu practically attacked me with sunscreen when we got on board." I couldn't help the laugh that escaped. Zu had been wearing a sports bra and a pair of shorts. She had made sure to spray both Gabby and me with sunscreen and then requested we do the same to her.

"Then I guess I'll head back down and help Zu. Silas is in his element up there on the fly bridge." He pointed to the raised area behind us.

"I was wondering what that was because there's a place to pilot the boat in the cabin, as well."

"It's standard. In case of foul weather or whatever. I don't know. You'd have to ask Silas. I know the fly bridge is good for fishing. It gives better visibility." He blew out a breath. "Anyway, I'm going to go help Zu."

"I'll come with you. I'd like to get a bottle of water. Claire, would you like anything?" Gabby accepted Oliver's hand and used it to rise to her feet.

"A sports drink would be nice. Blue if possible."

"You know they have names for the flavors, right?" she asked.

"Yes. Red, blue, yellow, green. Those are the names." I stuck my tongue out at her.

"Don't make promises." She pointed a finger at me and wagged it. "I'll be back in a minute."

"No rush."

The water around Bayview was not pretty. It's brackish, a mix between the saltwater from the Gulf of Mexico and the freshwater of the local rivers. It's all bracketed in between a line of barrier islands and the coastline. It didn't make pretty vistas, but it did make for good shrimping.

I was wondering how to mix shades of gray and brown to get a proper representation of the water when I noticed fins appear in the water. I got up and walked closer, sitting down on the edge of the boat, allowing my legs to swing over the sides under the rail. The rail was the right height to rest my arms and chin on, and I did so to get a better look at the dolphin pod.

Dolphins had always been my favorite water animal. I remembered seeing them at the old aquarium on class trips. They would feed them and have the dolphins perform tricks. I remembered feeling sad that such intelligent creatures were forced to perform for food, like the trapped humans in an alien zoo some science fiction writer created. I remembered reading a lot of sci-fi in high school. I had been addicted to shows dealing with space or the paranormal.

Something clicked in my head. I understood then why I had thrown Mr. Hawkins into the role of villain and who had helped feed that delusion. It had all gone back to that Halloween photo in the yearbook.

"What's going on?" Gabby asked as she joined me.

"Dolphins. Those are dolphins, right?" I wasn't ready to face that yet. There was more information I needed. I didn't just want to accuse a man without having something concrete.

"Come on, Claire. Seriously."

"Lighten up." I knocked my shoulder into hers. "I'm teasing."

"You are one of a kind, you know that, right?"

"I thought I was a goober." I took the drink she offered and shook it a few times before opening and taking a long sip.

"Oh, you are that, as well." She took her sunglasses off her shirt and put them back on. "I remember how much you love dolphins. You painted them a lot in high school. Do you have any paintings or drawings left from then?"

"I have no idea. I'd have to ask my mom." I didn't look away from the dolphin pods. "For a long time, I'd painted the madness in my head. Anytime I tried to do a still life or a landscape, it felt wrong. It was like I had forgotten how to see the beauty in things."

"I can't imagine what that's like."

"I'm not healed, not by a million miles, but I can sense the light at the end of the tunnel or whatever cliche is appropriate." I pulled out my phone, surprised I still had cellphone coverage. "Weird. I have a signal."

"Oliver said we should have it all the way out on the island, though it might fall into an old roaming category. Calls might be expensive, like if we were international."

"That's good to know." I flipped to the camera and began taking video of the dolphins. "If things go like they did the other time then we may need that."

"Do you remember anything?"

"Not really. We're not there yet." I turned the camera on her. "Smile, beautiful."

"You gathering resources for your next series of paintings?" Zu asked as she appeared and sat down next to me. "I wanna be in one."

"Oh, sure. I'll get an easel and move to New Orleans and make portraits of tourist for fifty bucks a pop." I turned the phone in her direction to capture her reaction.

"Well, that would keep you supplied in cardboard boxes for you to live in," she countered.

"Silas said we're going around the island like we did the first time and it's going to get bumpier," Gabby informed us.

"The water's blue on that side, isn't it?" I asked.

"Yes, it is. The waves are bigger, as well," Zu answered.

"Hang on, I'm speeding up." Silas's yell was barely heard. I waved in acknowledgement.

We stayed on the bow as Silas piloted the boat around the tip of the island. It was a whole different world on the other side. The water was clear and blue. The waves were taller and white capped. We had lost the dolphins but gained a following of seagulls.

"Getting ready to anchor," Silas called as the boat slowed down.

"Do you need us to do anything?" Gabby asked.

"Nope. Just sit there and look pretty," he hollered back.

There was a grinding noise behind us and almost below us. There was a splash. I leaned forward a little to see the anchor line.

"We're pretty far away from the island. How are we going to get there? It looks deep," Zu said.

"Let's go find out." Gabby stood up first. I needed her help. Zu didn't. "Be careful. No one needs to get in the water before we all do."

"Yes ma'am."

It was not easy to walk back to the deck from the bow without going through the cabin. I walked almost like I was marching, foot in front of foot, rolled heel to toe. The railing wasn't tall enough to use as a hand hold, so I kept one hand on the boat itself.

"Anyone want to lend a hand?" Oliver was releasing the dingy from the swim platform. "We're gonna take a smaller boat to the island."

"Do we have to row?" I asked. I was not prepared to do that. It seemed like way too much work.

"Nah, it has a motor," Silas told us as he came down the ladder from the fly bridge. "We are now anchored securely and ready to head there. Let's load her up. Oliver, you have it fully in the water?"

"Aye, Captain."

"Smart ass." Zu started pulling an ice chest closer.

It didn't take long to load the dingy, which had a hard bottom but inflatable sides. We had two ice chests, a few folding camping chairs, two tents and a few bags of food and stuff. Once the five of us were in there, too, it was very tight fit. I honestly didn't think we would make it without sinking, but we did.

Chapter Twenty-One

"This is about where we were found. Spark any memories?" Silas waved his arm around the beach.

"No, it doesn't." I couldn't answer honestly and say that it may have. I wasn't sure. Something was tickling the back of my brain, but I had no idea what it was.

"Give her some time, asshole. We just got here."

"Why are you so protective of her, Gabby? She broke your heart too."

"I what?" I shielded my eyes with my hand and looked at her. "Did I?"

"Claire, it doesn't matter right now, okay? Ignore Silas. He's being *disparatado.*"

"Gabby, are you swearing in Spanish again?" Oliver wiped his hands on his pants. "Calm yourself, Chica. Come help us put up these tents."

"Yeah. Sure. Claire, after this, we'll talk, okay?" She placed a soft hand on my arm and squeezed gently.

"Yeah. Okay." I looked around. Silas had gone to help Zu put up the other tent. There were only two this time. We had three before, I think. "I'll go gather firewood."

I knew firsthand how very tangled and subjective a memory could be. I was also aware of how unreliable my memories were. The had put me on very powerful antipsychotics at seventeen. I had spent a total of five years, three months, and nineteen days in mental health treatment facilities. I had travelled, sought a higher power, gone to AA meetings, spent weeks in a dissociative state, and dropped acid. I was the last person on the planet to believe in the accuracy of memory.

However, I tried. I owed it to myself, to my friends, to Gwen and to Mr. Hawkins to try. So, as I collected deadfall, I relaxed my brain and let my thoughts drift. This wasn't something I did often because the places my brain could go scared me.

The island had a peculiar smell. There was the scent of pine, the passive odor of sand, the salt water in the air, and something else I had never been able to define. It was comforting and terrifying at the same time.

I knew almost instinctively that our other visit to the island had not been our first. Growing up when, how, and where we did, a lot of kids learned to pilot a boat before they learned to drive a car. Most parents trusted their kids more in the open water than they did on the open road. No matter the socioeconomic background, it was universal here. boating was good, fishing was life.

By the time I had gathered enough wood for a decent fire, the others had finished setting up the tents and getting the coolers from the boat. I watched it bob for a moment, tethered to the shore by a rope and a piece of metal and felt something stir in me.

"You okay?" Gabby's hand was light on my shoulder. "We're gonna need more wood. I'll help you gather more."

"Thanks." With my attention off the boat and back on my surroundings, I forgot what I had almost remembered.

Silas was our resident pyromaniac, so he stayed behind to make fire while the rest of us gathered more wood. It was weird with the five of us. The dynamic was off. There wasn't as much teasing and laughter as there had been. Gwen's absence was a shadow that still affected us all, even all these years later.

"Silas shouldn't have a problem getting a fire started with the wood you got already. I just figured we'd run through wood fairly quickly. Do you remember his habit of tossing lit newspapers in the park and hoping to start a forest fire?" Oliver asked.

"Why were we friends with him again?" Zu muttered.

"You wanted to fuck him." I was certain that was true.

"Did you guys ever?" she asked. Gabby and Oliver stopped and looked around at me.

"I don't think so. I'm not f sure, but I'm pretty positive we never did." I looked around at them. "Wouldn't you guys know? We would have talked about it, right?"

"You never said anything to me about it, but that doesn't mean you didn't do it," Gabby answered.

"He always said you did, but Silas does tend to lie about things." Oliver picked up a large branch. "This should be enough. We can always go looking for more as needed."

"Wait a minute, Silas always said Oliver was the liar." I pulled Gabby closer. "I'm so fucking confused."

"I imagine so. Claire, I know this isn't easy for you. It's not easy for us either, but none of us were with Gwen when she vanished. There's a good bet you were. Look, we'll talk about all this later. Let's get back. I'm getting thirsty. It's easy to forget how dry the saltwater makes everything." She patted my arm. "Come on."

"Okay."

I followed them back to the campsite with an armload of wood and a head full of buzzing. In art, in photo manipulation, in image creation, there's a technique of creating layers with various opacities. My mind felt like that, like it was struggling to make a whole picture out of various layers with differing levels of opaqueness, different mediums. Some I could see clearly, like acrylic painted on thick and bright. Others, I could only see the outline, softer watercolors hinting at movement. Some I couldn't make out at all, but I knew they were there, like the outlines of a rough sketch.

"And Prometheus gave man the gift of fire. I give it to you," Silas announced as we returned.

"Are you comparing yourself to a Greek god now?" Zu asked.

"A Titan punished by Zeus for an unselfish act," he corrected. "I have no such lofty goals."

"Well, I'm hungry. Let's get some food on this fire." Oliver put his sticks down and pulled one of the ice chests closer.

"Excellent." Zu began setting up the chairs. "Gabby, I wasn't sure what you would want, but I did find these." She tossed Gabby a bag.

"You found vegan marshmallows? Oh my god, you are awesome!" I had not seen her so happy in very long time. "Claire, you have to try these."

"Fine, but can I use regular chocolate?" I grabbed two bottles of water from the other ice chest and sat down in one of the chairs by the fire. "Got you a water."

"Thanks." She took the chair next to me. "Oliver, we got sticks for roasting shit. They're somewhere around here. Claire got aluminum foil, as well."

"I got premade sandwiches as well as a vegetable tray. I don't cook much," Zu told us.

"I got chips, hotdogs, marshmallows, chocolate, graham crackers, pineapple cubes, and corn on the cob. It's good if you leave it in the husk and set it near the fire for a few hours. Potatoes are good like that too, but I didn't want to deal with the sand."

"Do you do a lot of camping, Oliver?" Gabby asked. "That's quite a lot of stuff."

"I do actually. I don't tent too much anymore. Sleeping on the ground is not as fun or comfortable as it was in my twenties. I have a small bumper pull trailer. I try to use it as much as possible," he answered.

"I'm not one for nature," I told them.

"Hotdog?" Oliver passed one impaled on a stick. "Should probably eat something that appears to be food before you load up on chocolate and other sweet stuff."

"Thanks." I took it and held it above the fire.

As the others talked of small things, local sports teams, a little gossip, favorite TV shows, and so forth, I sat quietly and looked at them each in turn. Clearly one of us was hiding a secret. One of us had been responsible for Gwen's disappearance.

Oliver's behavior since our talk at my mother's house had been very different toward me. He had been kinder, more solicitous. It matched the attitude he had back in high school from what I could remember. Gwen had always said how well he treated her. He didn't push her. He respected her boundaries. I wonder if it had gotten to be too difficult to do so and he snapped.

Gabby was her usual self. She had always been my biggest supporter and cheerleader. That hadn't seemed to change. She had believed in me when I had no idea who I was. I could never repay her love and loyalty, though I had discovered the desire to try. She was a nurse and had a deep love for the environment and the rights of others. Was there a chance that stance had been created out of a need to right a wrong? To atone? I doubted it, but I couldn't rule it out completely.

Zu had always been kind, smart, and funny. That seemed as true now as it had been then. She was the smartest of us. She was incredibly logical and one of the last people I would ever suspect to harm a friend. Zu had been interested in Silas at the time, she had admitted as much. There was no reason for her to accost Gwen, who had been dating Oliver. It didn't mean it happened, but it was the least likely scenario.

Silas. I wasn't sure what to make of Silas. His behavior had been odd, to say the least. It didn't mean he did anything wrong, but the picture I had defaced in the yearbook suggested that at one time I was angry at him. I remembered that night at Mr. Hawkins's house. He had played into my delusions. Of that I was pretty sure of now. I also got the feeling that he enjoyed trying to gaslight me. He always talked around things and hinted at stuff and then denied doing so.

And then there was me. There were gaps in my memory for sure. I suffered from severe post-traumatic stress disorder. Three out of five former therapists agreed with that. I knew from my own research and various diagnoses that severe trauma could cause a type of amnesia. I have always wondered if that gap in my memory and the instability it revealed or caused was because I had killed my best friend. I could think of no motive, but to paraphrase, there was always some bullshit reason to kill your best friend.

"Claire, you still with us?" Oliver asked.

"Yeah, I'm here." I looked down and realized my hotdog had caught on fire and so had the stick. "Shit." I tossed both into the fire.

"Here, take this one." Zu handed me the one she had cooked. "I'd rather hold out for one of those corn things Oliver is making. I've always kinda worried that I'm not eating meat when I eat a hotdog."

"It's because of that book we had to read in American literature with Ms. Scarposi." Silas opened a beer. "Anyone else want a drink? Claire?"

"No. Thanks, though." I heard Gabby almost growl. "I'm okay."

"I'll take one." Oliver held up his hand and Silas tossed him a can.

"Me, too." Zu caught a can, tapped the top a few times and opened it.

"I'll stick to water, thanks," Gabby said.

"Scared there's animal piss in my beer, Gabby?" Silas asked.

"Not at all. A lot of American beers are vegan, asshole."

"Silas, why have you been so combative?" Zu asked.

"I haven't been combative." He took a long sip of beer. "Maybe I just don't enjoy being back here."

"How did you know this was the spot or roughly thereabouts?" I was curious. "Do you still come out here?"

"Yeah, you obviously still boat. Where do you go when you take that thing out? It's yours, isn't it?" Oliver sat his beer in the cup holder and leaned forward.

"This boat? Yeah, I suppose it's mine. I'm the only one who uses it. Is that suspicious? That I still boat? Man, I love deep sea fishing. It's very relaxing."

"Weren't there wolves here at one time?" Zu asked. "I remember one of you guys trying to scare us with a story about wolves being free on the island."

"That's a rumor. There's several of them about this place. The ruins of a building that people say was a government research installation are there. There's old cabins half destroyed by hurricanes that were supposedly someone's boneheaded idea of a resort." Oliver threw another branch on the fire. "I grew up hearing all those rumors."

"Okay, so I remember we had a campfire like we do now. Right?" I looked around to see them nodding at me. The sun was still up. We still had an hour or two before sunset. "And we had three tents?"

"Right. Since the boat we used didn't have a cabin, we all decided to sleep on the island," Oliver said.

"Where was the boat?"

"It was anchored just offshore here. We couldn't beach it like we did the dingy," Silas answered.

"Watercolor ghosts." I wasn't sure I said it aloud until I looked up and everyone was staring at me. "Watercolor fades easily unless you use expensive paint and take all the precautions. I feel like that's what I'm looking at, a faded watercolor landscape full of ghosts."

"Claire, I know this can't be easy for you. I'm sorry. I really am." Oliver leaned forward in his chair with his arms crossed on his thighs. "I would love to say for us to take a break and talk about it all later, but I can't. You and Silas are the only two who know what happened to Gwen. At least one of you does and I think it's long past the time we found out."

Chapter Twenty-Two

"What do you mean?" Zu asked.

"Oliver really?" Gabby protested.

"I know. You're right." When I said that, I was completely calm. I believed him, as well. "I've remembered some things and done a lot of thinking now that my mind is relatively clear. You're so right. It was either Silas or me. Or both."

"What the hell makes you think that?" Silas didn't raise his voice. It was calm. Eerily so.

"Because Zu absolutely had no motive. Gwen and Oliver were devoted and sleeping together. Gabby had no motive that I can see. But I don't remember if I did it or not. And Silas, there's something that's not right about you. I can't remember why or what for, but I don't trust you."

"Get off it, Claire, we dated. Hell, I was your first. Why would I kill your best friend?"

"We never slept together, though. I'm pretty certain of that. In fact, when we got our updated vaccines for college, I remember the nurse asking me if I was pregnant and telling her it would be a virgin birth if I was." I put down the hotdog on a stick I had been holding. I hadn't even taken a bite of it.

"There was a storm that night. Do you remember that?" Zu prompted.

"No. I remember only pieces of how we got here, and some of that just started coming back."

"So, let's start the story as we know it. Each of us will fill in the gaps for those who have them," Gabby proposed. "We got here. We walked from the boat to the shore carrying what little supplies we had in those days on our heads to keep them from getting wet. It wasn't supposed to rain, but you remember how accurate the weather guys used to be, right? Anyway, we set up camp and goofed off for a while. Sat around the campfire trading stupid stories. The guys tried to fish for dinner."

"That was part of the point. We were supposed to be on a fishing trip, me and Silas. You girls were supposed to be camping at Claire's uncle's farm."

"That's why they didn't miss us immediately. We weren't all supposed to be together," Zu explained. "Before the storm came up, we were drinking here by the fire. You and Silas went off somewhere, and then you came back, but he didn't. You were upset, but you sat down next to Gabby and me and started drinking, too."

"What were we drinking?" I asked. I was trying to envision it.

"Wine coolers and beer. The only things we could beg, borrow, or steal," Silas answered. "I had some pot, too. We smoked that off and on."

"So, we were drunk and stoned on an island with little in the way of supplies, and a convenient storm." Oliver laughed. "Typical teenage stupidity."

"If there was a storm, what happened?"

"We didn't really put the tents up well. They got blown down. Of course, we didn't go in them until the weather started getting bad. Once that happened, we looked for shelter elsewhere."

"One of the stories Gabby mentioned earlier was about the cabins," Zu explained. "Oliver grabbed a flashlight, and we ran into the woods to find them. When we got there, Silas and Gwen weren't with us. You went to go look for them."

"Which is why we know it had to be one of you. The three of us were together. Now when you and Silas joined us sometime around dawn, he claimed you hadn't seen Gwen, but Claire said you were pretty incoherent. You were also bleeding. I admit I was stoned, but I remember seeing that." Oliver leaned back in his chair.

"I left the three of you in the middle of a storm and went to go find Silas and Gwen? And Silas and I had gone off for a talk, but I had come back to the campfire. Where was Gwen then?" I was trying to picture it.

"In our tent with me," Oliver answered. "We were fooling around, about to do it, when Gabby and Zu must have heard us because they started catcalling. Gwen got embarrassed. We joined you guys at the campfire."

"Silas, where were you?" Gabby asked. "You've been awfully quiet. Anything you want to share?"

"I was exploring part of the island. I had talked to Claire for a few minutes and then I went to see if I could find that government place. No one else had wanted to go with me."

"I don't believe that," Oliver said.

"Me neither." Something struck me then. "Silas, you and I had broken up and you were mad about it, weren't you? You were stalking me, weren't you? I remember. I remember calls that used to wake us up at all hours, but no one spoke. We got dead flowers and stuff on the front porch. Oh, my God, did you kill Frohike?"

"Who the fuck is Frohike?" Zu asked.

"My dog. He was five. He was in perfect health, and we came home to find him dead. My dad always said he thought it was poison." I felt sick to my stomach. "You sick bastard."

"You've got a vivid imagination, Claire." Silas laughed. He laughed for a long time. "You think I killed your dog? Next, you're gonna say I killed Gwen, too!"

"Did you?" Oliver asked.

"No! But it's time to tell you all the truth. I've been covering for Claire. I'm sorry, but they deserve to know." He sat back and crossed one leg on the knee of the other. "Claire and I had an argument. That's true. I wanted to get back together. I loved her. She refused. I went off alone to nurse a broken heart. It was raining pretty hard by the time I got back. I went to check the boat, to make sure it stayed anchored. I heard Gwen and Claire arguing."

"What were they arguing about?" Gabby spoke up for the first time in a while.

"Claire was in love with Gwen, didn't you know?"

"No," Gabby said.

"Really?" Oliver asked.

"Who wasn't?" Zu commented.

"I what?" I tried to look at his eyes, to get a sense of why he was saying what he was, but night was falling, and he was in shadows.

"You came on to her. She freaked and threatened to tell your parents. You panicked and hit her with one of the thicker branches we had gotten for the fire. She yelled. I ran up there and stopped you, but Gwen had wandered out into the water. I couldn't find her. She was gone."

"No. That's bullshit." I knew that without a doubt. I thought back to the yearbook I had found. "I was never in love with Gwen. I know that for a fact. She and Hawkins were the only ones who knew I was attracted to girls. Before I broke up with you, I told her. I remember that clearly. I was in love with a friend, but it wasn't her and it certainly wasn't you."

"So, if that's true, and I'm inclined to believe Claire, that makes you the killer, Silas. So how and why did you do it?" There was a strength I had never before heard in Oliver's voice.

"The truth, Silas," Zu said.

Gabby took my hand in hers and held it tight.

"Come on, Claire." Silas got up, walked around the fire. "You can remember. For a while, you did. You had nightmares. You had the hallucinations. Those were manifestations of your guilt.

"What? No!" Everything dropped off. It all went black. All I could hear was Silas's voice.

He was so persuasive. I could see it, just the way he described. It was like watching an old horror movie, but distorted and cartoonish. I saw myself walk through the rain, struggling a little in the wet sand. It didn't feel right. It didn't hit right. The image was ruined from the start because it was completely false. There was absolutely no truth in it.

"Are you still doubting it?" His voice was closer. I opened my eyes to see him kneeling in front of me.

"I didn't kill Gwen." I flinched when he put his hands on my thighs.

"What do you think you're doing, asshole?" Gabby was on her feet in an instant.

"Why do you always protect her?" He sat back on his heels and looked up at us. "All of you do. Claire is not innocent! How many lives does she have to wreck before y'all see that? The Crosbys, Gabby's, her mother and father's, mine, April's, Justine's. How many more? Who's next?"

"Wait a minute, how do you know about Justine? Or April for that matter?" I knew there was a lot I didn't remember, but I greatly doubted ever telling him anything about the people I dated.

"You do seem to know a lot about Claire's personal life, Silas. Why is that?" Oliver asked.

"We keep in touch. She calls me sometimes when she's having a hard time, don't you, Claire?"

"No. You always call me. Do you honestly think I would call you? You have done jack shit for me. Gabby is the only one I've kept up with and that's mostly because she refused to let me just slink off and disappear."

"And why did you just want to disappear? Huh? Because you were guilty. Part of you has always known that, no matter how hard you try to bury it."

"No." He looked so strange, kneeling in the sand. The fire was behind him. Even though the sun wasn't completely down, he was mostly a silhouette .

"Why are you so intent on making Claire the villain?" Zu asked. If that was her courtroom voice, I was impressed.

"Fuck off, Zu. What are you going to do, put a flashlight in my face and try to intimidate me into telling you what you want to hear?" He scrambled to his feet and almost ended up in the fire. "So, what do you want to hear?"

"How about the truth for once?" Oliver got to his feet. "We found the cabins. Me, Zu, Gabby, and Claire. You went to check the boat. Gwen never showed. Claire left. The two of you found us hours later. Hours. Gwen disappeared and the boat was gone."

"What's your point?" Silas sounded bored.

"Silas, man, we all know you did it. We just can't prove it."

"Damnit, Oliver," Zu said.

"Can't prove it, but you *know*?" Silas laughed. He sounded unhinged. "Goddamn you fuckers! Someone died when we were kids and you just can't let it go."

"We were out here for three days, man." Gabby took a step toward him.

Silas walked to the other side of the fire.

Gabby continued. "The storm ruined what supplies we did have. Claire was damn near catatonic the whole time. We didn't have food or water. Now I've got my own ideas about what happened, but I think it's time you told us just what happened."

"For fuck's sake, Claire's found a new lease on life and to make her feel better about being slap ass nuts, we're all supposed to continue this farce?" Silas didn't look at me. His words felt like a slap.

"This conversation has gone on way too long. Silas, please? What did you do?" I don't know. Maybe I thought I would get through to him. He did claim to love me once. Maybe that still meant something.

"You're right, Claire. It has gone on too long." He reached around behind his back and pulled something from his pants. "Good luck getting out of here now, assholes."

"What are you doing?" Oliver yelled.

"Stranding you here again." Silas aimed the gun at a point behind us. I dropped to my knees in reflex. I don't think I was the only one either.

Two shots rang out and there was a loud pop behind us in the water. I looked back and saw a gaping hole in the inflatable boat. It was losing its air. We would have to swim out to the boat if we could.

"You assholes. You never got it. None of you. Who cares if some interfering bitch died out here decades ago? So what? No one is ever going to find her. She's sleeping with the fishes. Probably eaten by the fishes, literally."

"You mother fucker," Oliver growled.

"You'll never know now." Silas laughed again as he raised the gun and aimed it at his own head. "Catch you on the flip side."

"No!" I don't know who yelled. I think we all did.

I do know that time slowed down for once. Oliver and Gabby tore across the sand and threw themselves at Silas. Oliver made it first, but not before the third shot rang out, echoing like thunder.

Chapter Twenty-Three

"He's alive," Gabby said. "Get me something to stop the bleeding."

"What happened?" Zu asked as she pulled a beach towel from her bag. "Take this."

"Thanks. It looks like Oliver hit his arm, knocking off his aim. He shot himself, but he'll survive. I don't know if he'll be able to fully recover or not, but he's not going to die."

"Good." Oliver rolled and sat up. "He needs to stand trial and pay for what he did."

"This was not a good idea." I sat down in the sand and looked at my best friend taking care of my high school boyfriend. Damn, it was surreal.

"I'm calling the cops." Zu pulled her phone out of her pocket.

"This is a fucking disaster." Gabby pulled Silas's head closer to her. "Claire, go through the bags of food and other supplies. I'm going to need water and something to keep his head off the sand. Oliver, can you build up the fire? I don't want him going into shock."

"We have a rubber mallet, a few tent stakes, some fucking bonfire stick things, and assorted foods and beverages. We're so fucked." I rummaged through the bags beside the chairs and pulled out a bottle of water. I gave it to Gabby, trying not to look at Silas.

"This is not good. This is not what I expected." Oliver pulled the ice chests closer and to one side of the fire and sat down on one of them.

He motioned for us to do the same. "These aren't huge, but they'll give us some way to reflect the heat back on him."

"Claire, grab one of the sleeping bags. We can fold that up and put it under him to keep him out of the sand." Zu folded the chairs back up and put them on top of the ice chests Oliver wasn't sitting on. "I called the cops. They're supposed to contact the coast guard. Now we just need to wait. Do you think he's really going to make it?"

"Yes, but what I want to know is what Oliver meant." Gabby scooted closer. The four of us were huddled on the sand between two ice chests, the fire, and Silas.

"Yeah, Oliver, what did you mean?" I asked.

"I'll tell you in a minute." He got up, but never to his feet, and walked on his knees to the dingy. "Can one of you help me put this behind the ice chests? I'd feel better with a little more shelter."

"Yeah, I'll help." Gabby crawled beside him.

"You're so butch," I teased.

"It's nice to see you've got your sense of humor back," Zu said as we watched Gabby and Oliver manhandle the dingy into position.

"It's either that or break into that beer in the cooler we're hiding behind." I really wanted a drink. Like, I felt my body's cells cry out for booze.

"The boat's still here, but I don't think we're going to be able to get to it easily," Oliver said as he rejoined us. "Did the cops say how long it would take?"

"I don't even know if they believed me. Still, they said they'd contact the Coast Guard. I suppose we can always flag them down if a boat comes by."

"That's better than nothing. Smart idea, Oliver, making sure we could sit between the fire and the improvised barricade. It's gonna get cool tonight." Gabby rubbed her arms. "Now explain."

"When we made plans to come out here this time, I wanted to get Silas to confess. I'm sorry, Claire, I knew it wasn't you. I've known that for a long time. That little shit is slippery, though. I've asked him a few times, either plied him with alcohol and drugs, or just straight up asked. He always, always, no matter what, sticks to that bullshit story he gave the cops. You wandered out to find him, were out of it by the time you did, and he got you to us when the rain slacked off, and neither of you saw Gwen." Oliver took a very deep breath and exhaled loudly. "He heard screaming, but he thought it was just the wind."

"Tonight's the only time he's mentioned anything else?" Zu asked. "Yep."

"Why did you suspect him? I mean, I suspected myself for a very long time," I said.

"Honestly, I thought for some time that you were either covering for him or you were in it with him." He reached and patted my leg. "He always went on about how crazy you were and seemed to hint that maybe it was all an act."

"My mom said he visited me in the, you know, place. I don't really remember that too much. I do know that he played into my recent bout of paranoia when we broke into the Hawkins's house. He acted and reacted just like he was experiencing the same things I was."

"He did visit. I did, too. Zu went with me a few times. I've known for a long time that you didn't remember that. You were so far gone. They kept misdiagnosing you so then you weren't on the right meds. And then your father got the bright idea to get you put in the care of an evangelical psychiatrist who specialized in conversion therapy." Gabby put her arm around me. "The nineties weren't that open minded unfortunately, and we did live in Mississippi. Your mom got you out of there as soon as she could."

"Fucking Silas. She said that someone had talked to Dad. It had to be him. They got along. I think Dad was more upset by my dumping Silas than anyone other than douchebag himself." I had to keep myself from going closer and kicking him.

"Silas was my best friend in school. But I don't think I ever really knew him. You remember Mr. Singh, our biology teacher? Silas was one of two kids in the class not allowed to tend to the mice and gerbils in the classroom. He always claimed it was allergies, but looking back, I don't think so. He wasn't allowed to have pets."

"Are you saying he's a sociopath?" Zu asked. "That makes a sick sense. He can be extremely charming when he wants to be, but it's all surface. We went out after the accident once or twice, but it wasn't anything. I mean he was very polite and nice to my parents, almost too polite, but when we were alone, he was withdrawn or too cheerful. He wasn't interested in sex, either."

"Now that is weird. He always talked a big game," Oliver said. "Gabby, do you by any chance have any cigarettes on you?"

"No. I don't." She took her arm from my shoulders and looked down. "I quit again. The perfect time to do it, it seems, but it's been a few days."

"You quit? Really?" I was touched though I had no cause, no right to be.

"Yeah. We have to learn to walk without crutches, right?"

"Are you two back together?" Zu winked at me. "Cause you're really cute together."

"That's true, you are. Gabby's small and fierce. You're tall and seemingly fragile, but you're not." Oliver laughed. "It's everyone's favorite trope."

"What?" I looked at him to see if he was making fun of me.

"I read a lot of Manga. Watch a lot of anime." He shrugged.

"You know." I looked at my watch. Not enough time had elapsed for a rescue, at least as I could make out. "The few times Silas would drop in or call or whatever, he'd tell me about you two. Kept calling Oliver a pathological liar and Zu a degenerate gambler. Hell, he even claimed Gabby was a hypochondriac."

"I'm a germaphobe, I admit that freely, but I do work in a very active ER in a very crime riddled city." Gabby rested her arm around my shoulders again. I leaned into the touch and warmth.

"I go to the casinos occasionally. My grandmother loves the buffets. We usually go at least once when I'm here."

"I'm not a pathological liar. Of course, even if I were, I would say that. I'm a bartender. My girlfriend owns the bar. It's called Wall Street. She's expecting our first child. None of that is bullshit. You can look it up. We have a webpage, reviews, social media, all of it."

"Call the cops again," Gabby suggested. "Oliver, you call them. Just tell them our boat broke down and we have a medical emergency. We can't let him sit there much longer. I've got the bleeding stopped, but he's going to need surgery to get the bullet out."

"Okay." Oliver pulled his phone out.

We sat in silence and listened as Oliver spoke to the cops. They patched him to the Coast Guard. He was on hold for a while. Finally, they agreed to send a boat out to get us. He did warn them about Silas. The rest of us stayed on lookout in case anyone else showed up.

It was surreal sitting there on the beach with a pitiful excuse for a barricade behind us to protect a mad man who could easily have killed all of us and who tried to kill himself. The wind was cold, the fire wasn't doing a whole lot to offset that. Gabby got up and covered Silas with one of the other sleeping bags.

"You know, this is almost funny when you think about it. There were six of us. Two were gay, four were straight, cis gendered, one was a sociopath. One is Black, one is Hispanic, and one was biracial and three are white. That grouping would drive a statistician crazy." Zu ticked it off on her fingers.

"I was never a fan of math." I fought back a yawn.

"Bored?" Gabby asked.

"Nope, just exhausted."

"Here." She crossed her legs and leaned back against the ice chests. "Lay down and snooze. We'll keep watch."

"Are you sure?" I didn't want to leave them with the responsibility. I felt as if it was my fault, all of it. If I hadn't broken up with Silas—but how was I to know he was a ticking bomb about to explode? I really needed a therapist.

"Absolutely." Oliver nodded his agreement.

I rested my head in her lap and closed my eyes. I took deep breaths, filling my lungs with the smell of saltwater, sand, pine smoke, and Gabby. For a moment I wanted to bottle that scent. I knew then what my next painting would be if we ever got home.

Home. That brought about other thoughts. My mother had found me a therapist. Seeing him would keep me on the coast. Maybe that was not a bad idea. I had no support in St. Louis. Lane was great, but he wasn't Gabby. I wondered for a moment if I could get Gabby to move back, as well. That was too much for me to think about as tired as I was.

I must have drifted off, because suddenly there were members of the Coast Guard talking to Oliver and Zu. I sat up and looked around. Silas was still laying in the same spot, covered by beach towels and sleeping bags.

"I guess the troops arrived in time?" I sat up and rubbed my eyes.

"Yeah. Come on." Gabby stood up and stretched before offering me a hand.

"Thanks. For everything."

"Ma'am? Do you have any injuries?" a young medic asked. He shone a light in my eyes and studied me.

"I'm fine. I just want to get home."

"I'm sure you do, Miss." A large, redheaded man took the medic's place in front of me. "Do you have anything to add about what happened?"

"I don't think so." I wasn't sure what Oliver and Zu had told them, but having heard Oliver's side of the phone conversation, I had a good idea. "Are you going to be able to save him?"

"Silas Brown?" the man continued when I nodded. "They've got him. Don't worry. Did you know this island is protected under the National Park Service? Use of a firearm is prohibited under national law."

"I didn't fire it."

"We are aware, Miss." He raised one hand to a button on his shirt and idly played with it. "Maybe I should start again. We are going to take the four of you back to the mainland. They're sending a chopper for Mr. Brown. We were on our way already. We had other calls about the gun shots. There's another group camping on the north side of the island."

"I hope they're safe." I felt sick to my stomach again. "Do you, um, do you need anything from me?"

"There are detectives from the Bayview Police Department waiting on you back at the dock."

"Thank you, sir. Gabby?" I turned to find her speaking to another member of the Coast Guard, but this one was a young, hot woman. For the first time in years, I felt jealousy blossom. "He said they're gonna take us home."

"Yeah, okay. I think Oliver's already on the boat." She patted the woman's arm. "I have your card if I remember anything else."

"She was cute," I said as we walked away.

"Yeah, but too short for my tastes. Oh, this water is going to be cold."

"It is."

The Coast Guard had brought one of their smaller boats as close as they could get without getting it grounded. We had to walk out to it. Gabby was right. The water was cold.

Chapter Twenty-Four

When we got back to the dock, there were a ton of EMTs, cops, parents, news cameras, and curious bystanders crowding around. The police had put up barricades that I recognized from Mardi Gras parades to keep most of the more eager ones back.

It was like a scene out of a movie. A young Coast Guard officer helped us off the boat. EMTs were waiting with blankets. Cops were circling, trying to get statements. Parents were rushing forward to hug us. Even Oliver's very obviously pregnant girlfriend had driven down. She was standing with his parents. It was a much better reunion than the other time.

"I was so worried. Are you okay?" my mom asked as she pulled me into a second hug.

"I'm fine, Mom. I'm okay." I hugged her back with as much vigor as I could. "We'll call Dr. Kamaal tomorrow. Can I stay with you?"

"You want to move home?" She laughed through her tears. "Absolutely. You are more than welcome."

"Thank you. We'll talk about it later. I need to speak to Gabby for a moment. I'll be right back."

It took me a moment to find Gabby. She was a hair taller than her mother, but shorter than her stepfather, brother, sister, stepsister, and sister-in-law. I walked toward them, stopping for a moment to wave at Oliver, who was hugging his girlfriend. They both had tears flowing. Zu was caught between her mother and grandmother. Her father was taking pictures with his phone.

"Gabby, can I talk to you for a second?"

"Sure." She turned to her family and made an excuse, promising to be back soon. "What's up?"

"I've decided to stay here. Mom found this psychiatrist, Dr. Kamaal. He's supposed to be pretty good."

"Good? Getting him to the college was a big deal. It was in all the papers. Apparently, he's like, renowned."

"Are you going back to Memphis?"

"Tomorrow. I have to."

"You could maybe, I don't know, move back here?" I was never smooth. Never.

"Claire." She sighed, grabbed my wrist, and pulled me farther away from the crowd. "It seems like I have been competing with a ghost since this happened. You can't toy with my emotions. I love you, yes. I always have, but I'm not here just as your safety net. I'm not your mama. And I'm not Gwen."

"I know that. I know that more than anything else I know." I looked as deep into her eyes as I could on a dark, cold dock in Mississippi. "I knew Silas was lying when he said Gwen and I fought because she turned down my advances or whatever. I knew that because I never loved Gwen. It was you. Gwen was never anything more than a friend or a sister. I love you. I always have. I just didn't realize it until I guess it was too late, that I still do. I never stopped."

"Claire." She had tears in her eyes.

"Do you know why I was looking forward to that stupid boat trip? After everything with Silas, with Frohike, with all of it?"

"I don't know. Same reason we all were? To celebrate that we were almost through with school?" She looked off toward the highway.

"No, it was so I could see you in a bikini, as stupid as that sounds. I didn't know what my feelings toward you meant. I just knew that I was frightened and excited. You got me in a way Silas never did. You understand me in a way no one else has ever done. If you ask April, you were the third person sleeping in our bed, not Gwen. You. I love you."

"Claire, I can't do this. I've got to get back to work. I have a job, and I have a life in Memphis. I know you plan on staying here. I think that's probably best for you. Dr. Kamaal is probably the best psychiatrist in the neighboring states. I think working with him is going to be great for you, but I can't just uproot my life.

"Okay, Gabby. You're right. I can't ask you to uproot your life. I don't know what anything means or what anything is going to become. I just know that being out there made me realize that you've been here since the very beginning, and I've never loved anybody else like I love you." I brushed a strand of her hair back. "Just keep that in mind, okay? You waited for so long. I can wait this time. I just needed you to know that."

"I have wanted to hear you say that for so long." She kissed my palm. "I just... let's do this. This is all I can do right now, okay? Give me some time. Let me go back to Memphis and keep my job. You stay here and get better. It'll be just like it was when you were in St. Louis."

"We'll talk?" I was scared. I didn't know where Silas was or what was going to happen next. I was worried that she would be tired of waiting. That she would get to Memphis and realize she was really hopelessly in love with a nurse or something.

"Of course. All the time. It will probably be easier to see one another since I do occasionally come home to visit my family." She smiled.

"So, what does that mean?"

"Honestly, Claire, it means I love you. I love you with everything I am, but I can't trust us right now. You need to get well. I've got some stuff to get past. I've waited for you for so long. I hate to have to ask this, but do you think you can wait a little for me?"

"Gabby, I will wait until the sun goes dark for you. Now go home, go back to work do what you need to do. I'll be here. I will always be here for you."

"Then I'm going to say goodbye now, okay? I'm gonna spend the rest of this night with my family. Tomorrow, I have to find a way back to Memphis." She leaned up and lightly kissed me. Her lips were soft and she smelled a little like the beach.

"Okay. I guess I'm gonna go home and make sure Mom didn't feed Vinnie a pound of bacon."

"That sounds like a plan. I'll call you, okay?"

"Yeah. Have a safe trip." I felt like crying again. This felt final and I didn't like that. At all.

I watched her walk back to her family. The crowd on the dock had mostly dispersed. As concerned as I was about what was supposed to happen next, I was too tired to worry about it, really. I just wanted a warm bed, a warm drink, and my cat.

"You ready to go? The lead detective said they'll call when they have news about Silas's condition. He's under arrest and under guard, but they're going to have to operate on him." I hadn't heard Mom approach.

"Yeah. Think we can have some of that hot chocolate from the other night?"

"Of course. I think a good plan would be pajamas, hot chocolate, possibly a shower, and that cat of yours on your lap. What do you say?

"I say that sounds perfect, Mom."

Chapter Twenty-Five

I didn't go to the sentencing. It was quite a relief to know the law found him guilty. I guess I still haven't processed everything that came out during his trial either. It's hard to believe that I thought I knew him, but on the other hand, he is responsible for a lot of my mental health issues.

I apologized to Ms. Hawkins again profusely. It's kind of wild, when I look back on it, that I turned an amazing, gentle man into a shadowy villain. I always blamed myself for not seeing through his evil façade easier and sooner, but it wasn't *his* façade I should've seen through. My current therapist is big on acknowledging past mistakes but not beating myself up for them. I mean, we talk twice a week. He reminds me constantly that it wasn't my fault. That I was just as much a victim as Gwen.

"Are you watching this?" my mother asked as she entered the room. The evening news was on. The ticker across the bottom was telling everybody how much time Silas got sentenced to.

"Not really. I'm just glad it's done."

"Well, maybe now you can finally, completely heal." She handed me a cup of hot chocolate before sitting in her chair.

"Yeah, hopefully." There had been a lot of tearful nights with my mother after we got back from the second trip to the island. She apologized. I apologized. We didn't mention my father. She had even gone with me when I went back to St. Louis, once, to officially move back down to Bayview. My lease had been finished for a while, and I had been going month to month, so that wasn't much of a problem.

No, the real problem was Gabby had left and not returned. We talked often on the phone. But I think she had her own healing to do. So did Oliver and Zu. We weren't ready for the revelations on the island, but then it's hard to be prepared to be emotionally devastated.

The three of them had come back for the trial, as we were all witnesses for the prosecution. The defense did try to badger me a little bit about my mental health issues, but after a while the judge had enough of it and put a stop to it.

Silas's attorney went so far as to call Stephanie to the stand about my meltdown in her house. She didn't help them much. It was good to see her. If nothing else, I owed her one hell of an apology. Fortunately, she accepted it gracefully. We would probably never be friends, but neither of us would duck if we saw the other coming.

"What do you want for dinner?"

"I don't know. Kind of tired of leftovers." Mom was a great cook, but I could only eat lasagna for so many meals before I wanted something different.

"Me, too. Do you wanna order pizza?"

"Sure." I looked at my mom as if she had grown another head. She wasn't often one to suggest ordering pizza. I was going to take full advantage of that. "Do you want me to order it?"

"Yeah, just give me one with everything on it except for sardines and pineapples."

"I don't I think they put sardines on pizza, Mom. I think it's anchovies," I told her as I pulled the app up on my phone.

"Oh, look at you, got your head back on right. Now, all the sudden, you're a know it all again. That makes me so happy." She smiled as she stood back up. "Let me know when the pizza gets here, I'm gonna be out back repotting my gardenias."

After I ordered the pizza, I grab the book Zu had recommended the last time I spoke to her. It was in the African futurism section. She was in love with the author. It was based in Nigeria. I was looking forward to it and found it quite interesting.

I was halfway through the fifth chapter of the book when I heard a car door slam. Vinny didn't move from my lap, so I had to ease out from under him. Thinking it was the pizza, I opened the door without checking first. That was something I had not done in a very long time.

"You look surprised to see me."

"Gabby!" I stood back to let her in. "You didn't tell me you were coming down."

"Yeah, I thought I'd surprise you." She closed the door behind her.

"It's a surprise." It was awkward for a minute. I didn't know if I should hug her or not. We had confessed our feelings but were still only friends.

"Is that the pizza?" Mom called from the kitchen.

"No, Mom, it's Gabby."

"Oh, hi, Gabriella. How was the job interview?" Mom peered around the doorframe.

"Job interview?" I turned to see a very surprised look on my friend's face. "You had a job interview?"

"Yeah, I was going to talk to you about that." She walked into the living area and sat down on the couch. "Come here."

"Okay." I was a little nervous. "What's going on?"

"I was thinking, with everything going on and how Silas finally got convicted. It sucks so hard that Gwen didn't get justice., But for everything else he's done, he'll be gone a long time. At least he recovered completely and was able to stand trial." She ran a hand through her hair.

"You're babbling. What's going on?" I knew her pretty well. She only babbled when she got nervous.

"I love you. You know I do. It's been tough being up in Memphis when you've been down here. A lot tougher than it was when you lived in St. Louis."

"Okay?" I prompted.

"I've been looking for jobs down here. I'm not happy at the hospital anyway. Just taking time off that they owed me was a painful reminder that I work for bastards." She sighed. "I don't want to get ahead of ourselves, okay?"

"What do you mean?"

"What I mean is that I'm thinking of moving down here. I thought we'd date. See what happens. You live here with your mom and keep seeing your therapist. I'll professionally establish myself here. We'll see what happens. Think that's good for now?"

"Absolutely. Dr. Kamaal wants me to strengthen ties with people who are good for me. He says I need to reinforce my support network. You're one of the biggest supporters I have. I don't want to fuck anything up with you. Again."

"Great. So, slow. Steady. Date. One thing at a time." She sighed and leaned back on the sofa.

"I'll get it," Mom hollered when the doorbell rang. "Gabby, you'll stay for dinner. We got pizza."

"Sure." She smiled and looked me in the eyes. "I'll be here."

"Me, too."

It was a wonderful evening spent with the two women I loved most. And Vinnie. We didn't know what the next day would bring. But we had one another. That was enough.

Afterword

This is a work of fiction, however, some of the issues Claire faces are very real to a lot of people. I try not to preach, but if you need help, please reach out.

Resources include:
The Trevor Project can be reached via Thetrevorproject.org

National Suicide Hotline in the US:
988 from any phone or 988lifeline.org

Alcoholics Anonymous has a lot of good information
and contact info at aa.org

Acknowledgement

Books don't write themselves, which is very unfortunate for writers everywhere. This writer in particular is indebted to two amazing editors; Jeanine and Sharon, my awesome publisher, Patty; and Christine, Kyla, and Kaleto, my beta readers.

I am also indebted to my amazing friends and support network, without which I can honestly say I would not be here. Darci, John, Tabitha, Dennie, Thom, Christine, and Kyla. I love you all.

This book is dedicated to my daughter, Emerson. Not all change is bad, and sometimes the end of one thing is the beginning of something better.

Bringing rainbow stories to life.

Flashpoint Publications welcomes submissions from writers
of every color and books featuring characters of every color.
In addition, Flashpoint Publications encourages job applicants
of every color whenever a staff position becomes available.
We believe that EVERYONE is entitled to a seat at our table.

www.flashpointpublications.com